Mr Daniel Cooper of Stickleback Hollow

The Mysteries of Stickleback Hollow

By C.S. Woolley

A Mightier Than the Sword UK Publication

©2017

Mr Daniel Cooper of Stickleback Hollow

The Mysteries of Stickleback Hollow

By C. S. Woolley

A Mightier Than the Sword UK Publication

Paperback Edition

For

Rach

Author's Note

Thanks for taking the time to read *Mr Daniel Cooper of Stickleback Hollow*, I hope you enjoy it, there is much more to come in the series if you do! As the third book in the series, this book picks up not long after All Hallows' Eve.

The Characters

Lady Sarah Montgomery Baird Watson-Wentworth

The heroine

Brigadier General George Webb-Kneelingroach

Guardian of Lady Sarah and owner of Grangeback

Bosworth

The butler

Mrs Bosworth

The housekeeper

Cooky

The cook

Mr Alexander Hunter

A huntsman and groundskeeper of Grangeback

Pattinson

An Akita, Alexander's hunting dog

Constable Arwyn Evans

Policeman in Stickleback Hollow

Doctor Jack Hales

The doctor in Stickleback Hollow

Miss Angela Baker

The seamstress in Stickleback Hollow

Wilson

The innkeeper in Stickleback Hollow

Mrs Emma Wilson

Wife of Wilson and cook at the inn

Mr Henry Cartwright

Owner of Duffleton Hall

Stanley Baker

Son of Miss Baker

Lee Baker

Son of Miss Baker

Reverend Percy Butterfield

The vicar in Stickleback Hollow

Mr Richard Hales

Son of Doctor Hales

Mr Gordon Hales

Son of Doctor Hales

Mr Daniel Cooper

A gentleman from Tatton Park

Mr Stuart Moore

A gentleman of Cheshire

Mr Jake Walker

A gentleman of Cheshire

Mr Thomas Egerton

Son of Wilbraham & Elizabeth

Mr Edward Christopher Egerton

Son of Wilbraham & Elizabeth

Lady Szonja, Countess of Huntingdon

Cousin of Elizabeth Egerton

Lord Joshua St. Vincent

A young lord in the employ of Lady Carol-Ann

Mr Callum St. Vincent

A young gentleman in the employ of Lady Carol-Ann

John Smith

An Alias

Lady Carol-Ann Margaret de Mandeville, Duchess of Aumale and Montagu

The villain

Chapter 1

Manners makyth man, and as such, there is never an excuse for a breach of etiquette. At least this is what Brigadier General George Webb-Kneelingroach had been brought up believing. He was a man that had been made by his days at Winchester and serving his country in the armed forces.

He had always prided himself on his manners and hospitality. It didn't matter to the brigadier where one had been born, but what one chose to do with the time that they had been gifted to walk upon the Earth.

This being said, the brigadier was not a man to suffer fools, scoundrels or wastrels. It was in this contradiction in his character that he now found himself torn.

Mr Daniel Cooper had taken up residence in Duffleton Hall, and as a new resident in the neighbourhood, etiquette demanded that the brigadier call upon his new neighbour and welcome him to the area.

Mr Daniel Cooper was not a stranger to Stickleback

Hollow or Grangeback as he had been residing at Tatton Park with his mother and the Egerton family since his father's death.

George had never had any call to doubt the character of Daniel until Lady Sarah Montgomery Baird Watson-Wentworth had become the ward of the brigadier. She was a young woman of fortune, vitality and was exotic compared to the famed beauties of England as she had passed her life in India until only a few months ago.

She had come to England after the death of her parents and became the ward of the brigadier as well as his heir.

Lady Sarah's presence at Grangeback had changed how the brigadier viewed all young men that he knew. He also now viewed interlopers into the neighbourhood with suspicion.

As far as the brigadier could tell, Daniel was swept up in Sarah's beauty and how different she was from the other women that he knew. The young man had already been bold enough to enquire into the lady's relationships to other young men of her acquaintance.

But George was wary of how easily infatuated young men and young women could become with one another. That as soon as that initial wonder had disappeared, there would be nothing but misery and pain left in its wake.

His own daughter had fallen prey to such an infatuation, and he was eager to prevent Sarah from making the same mistake.

By calling on Mr Daniel Cooper, the brigadier had to be careful to not indicate that he was giving any form of permission or invitation that would entice Daniel to pursue Lady Sarah, whilst still maintaining a polite and socially acceptable comradery with his neighbour.

"You should treat it as a chance to observe the young man more closely. You can hardly make a judgement on his behaviour at this point." Doctor Jack Hales had counselled his old friend.

"It is hardly the behaviour of a rational man to take an estate such as Duffleton after spending an evening with a woman that was filled with danger and intrigue." George snorted.

"I have yet to meet a man who behaves in a rational manner as far as women are concerned." Doctor Hales replied.

So the next day, the brigadier ordered his carriage to take him to Duffleton Hall. Sarah was still in bed when he left as she was still recovering from the injury she had received on All Hallows' Eve.

It didn't take long for his carriage to make its way down the narrow country roads that led from Grangeback to Duffleton.

Daniel welcomed the brigadier in the grandest fashion and spoke for hours about his plans for the estate. Lunch was prepared and served to the brigadier. Discussion between the two men went on well into the afternoon.

George found it amusing that Daniel was going to such great lengths to impress him, on what he could only assume was Sarah's behalf.

As her guardian, it was the brigadier's permission that Daniel would need in order to court and marry Sarah.

As the shadows had begun to lengthen, George had made his excuses and taken his carriage back to Grangeback. On his way back he took a slight detour to the lodge that lay just outside of Stickleback Hollow.

It was the home of Mr Alexander Hunter, a hunter by profession and the groundskeeper of the Grangeback Estate.

"What brings you out here so late?" Alex asked as George opened the door to the lodge. Mr Hunter was a man that observed a different kind of hospitality to most. Those that knew the man were well aware that his door was always open and guests were welcome in the lodge, whether the hunter was there or not.

There was never a need to announce their arrival or wait for an invitation to enter when visiting Mr Alexander Hunter.

Alex was sat at the table in his kitchen, fletching a new set of arrows when George walked in. Pattinson was lying in front of the fire. The great dog flicked his eyes in George's direction, but made no other effort to move.

"I went to call on Mr Cooper at Duffleton Hall," George replied.

"I would have thought you would have visited him in the morning," Alex said, without shifting his eyes from his arrows.

"I did, he kept me there all day," George yawned as he sat down in the chair opposite Alex.

"How does Duffleton look in the hands of its new master?" Alex asked.

"Well, not much has changed since Henry owned it, but then I would hardly have expected much to have changed in just a few weeks. He seems to have very big plans for the place though," George sighed and rubbed his temples.

"You don't approve?" Alex asked, looking up at George for the first time.

"Of progress - the so-called progress - he outlines I am sceptical of, to say the least. He seems more determined to sell off the estates and develop his home as an industrial centre than to farm the land and look after his tenants," the brigadier said disapprovingly.

"You can't control how other men use their land," Alex shrugged.

"No, but I can be wary of his attention towards my ward?" George replied gruffly.

"Sarah?" Alex frowned.

"No gentleman spends an entire day with an ageing neighbour, offering him lunch and telling him about his extensive plans for the future," George said with a raised eyebrow.

"I see your point. So his first attempt at impressing you has annoyed you?" Alex asked as he put down the arrow he was working on.

"He's too eager to impress me. Young scoundrels are

18

always too eager to impress," George said grumpily.

"Well, if he is, then you are her guardian. It's up to you to keep unworthy men from the door," Alex sighed.

George looked at the pile of arrows that Mr Hunter had fletched and frowned slightly. Though he had pistols, rifles and shotguns, Alex preferred to use a bow and arrow – especially when hunting. He was a tall and broad man that could easily handle a bow.

"Is there some problem that I am unaware of?" the brigadier asked slowly as he drew his eyes up from the arrows to Mr Hunter.

"I've been asked to go to Scotland. A gamekeeper, a friend of Old Mitchell, sent a telegram requesting some help," Alex explained.

"There's trouble in Scotland?" George made a face at the very idea.

"Apparently, the population of red deer is raging out of control, and there are a few gamekeepers who want my help advising the gentlemen on the matter," Alex shrugged.

"They can't do that themselves?" George laughed.

"I think they assume that a younger man from England will have more luck talking to the English landowners than tough old Scottish hunters," the hunter gave the brigadier a wry smile.

"Well, they clearly don't know enough about young English landowners. When are you leaving?" George asked.

"I was going to set out in the morning. The coach will take me as far as the border. From there I can take a local stage," Alex replied.

"Take one of my carriages. It will be more comfortable than any stage, and you can travel back whenever you are done without having to wait on the coaches," George smiled.

"Thank you," Alex said as he bundled his arrows together.

"I thought you would be more interested in Daniel's intentions towards Sarah. I know the two of you are very close," George said as he stood up to leave.

"We are from two different worlds; I am not going to stand in the way of what is best for her," Alex said sadly.

"That matters to you?" George frowned.

"It does," Alex replied.

"I see. Have a safe journey. I'll make sure that the carriage is ready for you," George said as he stood and left without another word.

When the brigadier reached Grangeback, he didn't feel like eating the dinner that Cooky had prepared for him. He didn't even want to eat a light supper.

"You seem to have had a long day," Sarah's voice greeted him as he stepped into the library.

The young lady was lying on one of the long sofas with a blanket thrown over her.

"You were supposed to stay in bed," George said disapprovingly.

"I was bored, and Mrs Bosworth let me come down to the library to read," Sarah smiled innocently.

"I see, then I am glad you are feeling better," George rubbed his face.

"Mrs Bosworth also brought a girl from Chester. She said that she was a lady's maid. She was living at a house in the city, but the family was ruined by a scandal. Mrs Bosworth knew the girl and knew I needed a maid, so she brought her to meet me," Sarah smiled, trying to take the brigadier's mind off whatever was bothering him.

"You finally decided to find a maid then," George replied as he sat in one of the large, high-backed, leather chairs.

21

"Mrs Bosworth and the other maids don't have the time to take care of me in this condition, and you wanted me to have one," Sarah shrugged.

"What was the scandal?"

"The master of the house lost the family fortune at cards and then took up with a rich widow to try and save his family from ruin," Sarah began.

"And the widow discovered this and exposed the scandal?" George asked.

"She did. The entire staff was laid off. According to Mrs Bosworth, most of them were hired by Daniel for Duffleton. But he didn't need a lady's maid," Sarah smiled.

"So is she an acceptable maid?" George didn't want to discuss Daniel Cooper with Sarah at this moment in time. He had had his fill of the young gentleman for one day.

"Grace, can you come in here, please?" Sarah called out. A young girl with blonde hair nipped into the library and stood next to the sofa that Sarah lay on.

She was thin and no taller than five feet. She looked petite and rather timid to be serving as Sarah's maid, but the brigadier felt relieved that Sarah would finally have a chaperone of sorts that would keep her out of dangerous situations.

"So this is Grace," George said, turning towards the lady's maid to look at her.

"Pleased to meet you, brigadier," Grace squeaked.

"Very good, well ladies, if you will excuse me, it has been a long and trying day," the brigadier said as he rose to his feet, "by the way, Mr Hunter is going to Scotland for a while. I am sure he would appreciate it if you could keep an eye on the lodge for him. Goodnight."

Chapter 2

The next morning, Sarah was awoken by the sound of the carriage being prepared by the stable hands. From her window, she could see Mr Hunter was down by the stables, helping to place the horses in the traces.

Pattinson sat beside the hunter, the dog was completely devoted to Alex and followed him wherever he went.

Harald was one of the team that was being put into the harness, which Sarah thought was odd. Even more odd was the groom putting Harald's tack into the carriage.

"Just how long is he planning to be gone?" Sarah asked herself. She chewed her bottom lip in thought as she watched the men work.

Before the four horses had finished being harnessed, Sarah had made a decision. She walked quickly from her room, without bothering to dress and descended to the kitchen using the servants' stairs.

She dodged through the milling maids and footmen.

24

She didn't stop when Cooky called out to her,

"Why are you down here and not dressed? Grace!"
Cooky yelled.

Sarah reached the backdoor and pulled it open. She moved as quickly as she could down the path that led from the kitchen to the stables.

The sound of the carriage doors shutting echoed from the stables before Sarah reached it. She could hear the driver cracking the whip and the carriage lurching forward.

She rounded the edge of the stables in time to watch the carriage leaving the stable yard.

"Mr Hunter!" Sarah shouted.

Alex leaned out of the window and looked back at the lady as she stood staring after him. For a moment, the hunter considered telling the driver to stop, but instead he nodded at Sarah and withdrew into the carriage. He resisted the urge to look back at her as the carriage trundled down the driveway.

Sarah didn't move as the carriage left. She stood completely still, her eyes fixed on it until it had vanished from sight. She felt hurt that he hadn't told her he was going anywhere and that he would leave without saying goodbye.

"My lady!" Grace panted as she raced into the stable

yard, "You must come back to the house. You are not dressed," the maid insisted.

"He didn't say goodbye," Sarah said, as though she were in shock.

"My lady, please," Grace begged.

"He saw me standing here. He didn't wave or say goodbye. He barely gave me a second glance," Sarah lamented.

Grace took Sarah gently by the arm and steered her back towards the house. Cooky clucked as Sarah was walked back through the kitchen, but instantly stopped when she saw that Sarah wasn't registering that Cooky was there, let alone listening to what she was saying.

"I'll make her some tea," Cooky said to Grace. Grace nodded and led Sarah back to her rooms.

The lady's maid took off her mistress' night things and replaced them with one of the dresses that Sarah had bought in London. She arranged and pinned Sarah's hair, then applied what make-up there was.

When she was done, Sarah looked like the quintessential Victorian woman of high society. Cooky came up with Sarah's tea and nearly dropped the tray she carried when she saw the lady.

"Oh my!" she cried," Mrs Bosworth, come quickly!"

A moment later, Mrs Bosworth bustled into the room and let out a cry of shock.

"Lady Sarah, whatever is wrong?" Mrs Bosworth asked as she knelt down next to Sarah, who was sat on one of the sofas in the room.

Sarah slowly turned her head to look at Mrs Bosworth, "He left without saying goodbye."

"My dear child, what a thing. I suppose Grace dressed you; that would account for it. Cooky, look after Lady Sarah. Grace, I will instruct you as to what her ladyship normally wears and does in a day," Mrs Bosworth said and led the lady's maid to Sarah's dressing room.

"Who left without saying goodbye?" Cooky asked as she set the tray down and began to pour the tea.

"Mr Hunter. He's gone to Scotland. He didn't tell me he was going, I saw the carriage leaving. I called out to him. He just looked at me," Sarah said sadly.

"Ah, I see. Don't fret child. That's just his way. He's always been gruff and closed off with everyone save for the brigadier. He's become a lot more amiable since you arrived

27

here, but I suppose that with the arrival of Mr Cooper in the neighbourhood, he's going back to his old ways," Cooky said as she handed Sarah a cup and saucer.

"Why would Daniel moving to Duffleton mean that Alex would go back to how he was before?" Sarah frowned.

"Because Mr Cooper is a gentleman and Mr Hunter is not," Cooky said gently.

"I don't understand," Sarah said, shaking her head.

"That's alright, child, I'm sure you will in time," Cooky smirked, but Sarah didn't see. The lady was looking down at her lap. She took a few sips of tea and seemed to come out of her state of shock.

"What am I wearing?" she asked as she realised that she wasn't in her nightgown anymore.

"Grace dressed you, don't worry, Mrs Bosworth is instructing her now. I'm sure that it won't happen again. Though, maybe this would be a good day to visit Chester. You are up nice and early, you certainly are dressed for visiting the city, and it would give you a chance to get away from this Mr Hunter and Mr Cooper nonsense for a while." Cooky suggested.

"I think visiting Chester is an excellent idea," Sarah said

28

brightly.

"And I daresay Grace will find it most interesting," Cooky grinned.

Mrs, Bosworth brought Grace back into the room and was glad to see Sarah looking better. She would find out from Cooky what had been bothering the young lady when they got back to the kitchen.

"Grace, we're going to Chester," Sarah announced as she set down the cup and saucer and stood up.

"Very good, my lady. I'll have one of the smaller carriages made ready," Grace said and hurried down to the stable.

"You know, I think she's going to be in for a terrible shock," Sarah said with a mischievous look on her face.

"She certainly was a little overwhelmed by your wardrobe, but she'll adapt, I daresay. Have you any particular plans in Chester?" Mrs Bosworth asked.

"Well, now that I have a lady's maid, she's going to need a horse," Sarah grinned.

"I see, are you sure that you are strong enough to go to the city? Only yesterday was the first time you had been out of bed since you were kidnapped," Mrs Bosworth asked with concern.

"The only reason I hadn't been out of bed before that is none of you would let me get out of bed," Sarah replied.

"Please be careful. We were all terribly worried about you. We don't want to see you back in the hospital," Mrs Bosworth said.

"I promise not to get kidnapped or shot in Chester," Sarah said glibly.

"I'm not entirely convinced that you will keep to that, but at least Grace will be there. I will tell the brigadier where you've gone," Mrs Bosworth said shortly and left the room.

Sarah chuckled to herself as Cooky cleared away the tea things.

"She means well. We all do," Cooky said disapprovingly to Sarah.

"I know. I'll buy her a new hat for church to apologise," Sarah sighed and left her rooms to head for the stables.

The journey to Chester took far too long for Sarah's liking. The coach was much slower than riding, though as Grace didn't have a horse, the carriage was their only means of reaching Chester.

Grace proved to be extremely useful in the city. She

knew where all the best shops were, the best places to eat lunch and where to avoid. It was a very different trip than Sarah's first trip to Chester had been.

On that occasion, she had been with Mr Hunter, trying to find the man who had robbed Sarah and attacked Bosworth, the butler.

It hadn't been all that long ago either. Sarah tried to put Alex out of her mind and focus on what she had come to Chester to do.

She went to a lot of different shops to buy gifts for all of the household, Doctor Hales and Constable Evans. They had all had a hand in taking care of her, and Constable Evans had risked his own life to save hers. Daniel and Alex had also risked their lives, but Sarah didn't feel it was necessary to buy Daniel anything, and after the way Alex had behaved, Sarah didn't feel inclined to buy him anything.

They visited the market and stopped by one of the inns to find a suitable horse for Grace. Grace felt uncomfortable the whole time they were inside the inn. There were a number of people that had their eyes firmly fixed on Sarah from the moment that she entered.

Sarah spoke to the innkeeper and was directed to an

older man in the corner. After half an hour, Sarah had struck a deal with the man and produced her purse.

Grace watched anxiously as a great deal of attention was directed at her lady. Sarah opened her purse and first produced her pistol. She placed it on the table firmly so that all in the inn could see it before she took out the coins to pay for the horse.

Grace almost fainted when she saw the pistol. She didn't know quite what to make of the woman she served. She had seemed to be so quiet and reserved the day before, but now. She carried a pistol in her purse, seemed completely at home in this dank and dirty inn, her choice in clothing bordered on scandalous, and she wasn't at all concerned about traipsing around the outdoors in her night things.

Sarah finished her business with the old man and returned to the innkeeper. She instructed him to have one of his stable boys take the horse to the inn where their carriage was waiting.

As they came out of the inn, a tall man, dressed in fine clothing collided with Sarah.

"My dear lady, my apologies," the young man took off his hat and bowed to Sarah.

"That's quite all right," Sarah said dismissively.

"Please, forgive me for being such a clumsy fool," the man continued.

"There is no need to be forgiven, it was an accident," Sarah said and tried to step past the man, but he blocked her path.

"You are too kind, dear lady. I am Lord Joshua St. Vincent. Might a humble creature such as myself be permitted to know your name?" he asked seizing hold of Sarah's right hand.

"Lady Sarah Montgomery Baird Watson-Wentworth," Sarah replied.

"Ah, the exotic beauty from India. You have caused a stir amongst the society of London. I was told that you were beautiful and charming, but the stories hardly do you credit. Would you perhaps do me the honour of dining with me this evening?" the young lord asked.

"I'm afraid I have a prior engagement, another time perhaps?" Sarah said lightly.

"But of course. I have taken rooms here for a few months. Please feel free to call on my anytime," Joshua smiled, kissed Sarah's hand and allowed the lady to pass. Grace trotted along behind Sarah, glancing back at the lord.

"Be careful with him, my lady," Grace whispered.

"What is it, Grace?" Sarah asked.

"He has something of a reputation. He trifles with women's hearts. He has led more than his fair share of women to their disgrace," Grace warned.

"Don't worry; I have no intention of ever seeing that man again," Sarah said firmly.

Lord Joshua St. Vincent watched Sarah and her maid as they walked down the street and disappeared around the corner.

"So that is the creature that has the duchess in such a flap," he chuckled to himself as he replaced his hat and set off in the opposite direction.

Chapter 3

Three weeks passed. Sarah kept herself busy by introducing Grace to her world and teaching the lady's maid what was expected of her.

Grace had never learned to ride, so after two days of learning about the house and Stickleback, the young girl was taught to ride.

She had come a long way in the three weeks that Sarah had spent teaching her. Every day for three hours in the morning and three hours in the evening, Sarah made Grace ride.

The first week was the hardest. Grace felt pain in muscles that she didn't know she had. As her muscles grew stronger, the pain lessened, and she found it easier to spend time in the saddle.

Sarah taught Grace to ride like a man. She didn't know how to ride side-saddle, and Miss Baker had to make some new clothes for Grace.

The lady's maid had quickly learned that in order to

serve as Sarah's maid, she would have to change how she dressed.

In those three weeks, the only visitor to Grangeback had been Miss Baker. The seamstress came to measure Grace for new clothes and then delivered them a few days later.

Sarah had expected Mr Daniel Cooper to come to call at least once; especially after the brigadier had spent so long at Duffleton Hall.

But Mr Cooper didn't come to call. There was no word from Scotland either. Whenever anyone mentioned Mr Hunter, Sarah would snort derisively, and the course of the conversation would instantly be changed.

Sarah had given all the gifts she had bought for the household to the recipients, and Doctor Hales had been thrilled with his gift, but Sarah hadn't taken Constable Evans his gift.

She waited until the first day of Advent before she went to visit the constable. Grace was given the day off to rest after spending a few painful weeks learning to ride.

Sarah saddled Black Guy and rode down to the village. There was a cold bite in the air that promised snow. Sarah wore her long riding cloak and a pair of long boots to try and keep out the worst of the cold.

As she rode down to the village, the snow began to fall in light flurries. The sky was covered with thick cloud, and the wind had started to rise. It was close to midday, but it was so dark that it seemed like it was closer to nightfall.

The lamplighters were already at work, making sure that the streets of Stickleback were lit as people tried to go about their daily business as the snow fell.

If the weather had been better, Sarah would have stopped at the inn, as it was, she didn't want to spend too long in the village in case the snowfall got heavier.

She rode straight to the police house, tied Black Guy outside and knocked on the door. Constable Evans made his way to the door and opened it.

"Lady Sarah, I didn't expect to see you," Arwyn said with surprise, "Is there a problem?" he asked as he welcomed her into the police house.

"No problem, save for this snowstorm. I came to bring you something." Sarah shivered as she stepped into the police house and went to stand by the fire.

"You brought me something?" Arwyn frowned.

"It's not much, but I wanted to thank you for coming to

37

find me on All Hallows' Eve," Sarah said as she pulled a parcel from under her cloak that was wrapped in brown paper and string.

"There's no need," Arwyn tried to refuse the gift, but Sarah pushed the package into the constable's hands.

It wasn't very big, but it felt heavy. Arwyn undid the string on the package, and the paper fell open to reveal a whistle and chain.

"I thought this might be useful," Sarah smiled.

The whistle and chain were both made from brass. The metal shone in the dim light as Arwyn tentatively picked it up and examined it.

"Thank you, it's perfect," Arwyn breathed. He was genuinely moved by the gift. It was clear that Sarah had thought about what Arwyn would need or find useful.

He had no need for baubles or decoration, but this gift was practical and would make him the envy of every other constable he would come across.

"I'm glad you like it," Sarah grinned.

"Sarah!" the door to the police house was thrown open, and Mr Hunter rushed in from the snowstorm. He looked pale as he came into the room and found Sarah stood by the fire with Arwyn still admiring his new whistle. Pattinson bounded beside his master.

"Mr Hunter?" Sarah replied.

"What's wrong?" Alex demanded, "What's happened?"

"Nothing. I came to bring Arwyn a gift," Sarah said with surprise.

"A gift? You came out in weather like this to bring Arwyn a gift?" Alex asked in disbelief.

"It wasn't snowing when I left. It was barely snowing when I arrived," Sarah frowned.

"Come with me," Alex said as he grabbed Sarah by the arm and marched her out of the door.

Sarah tried to resist, but Mr Hunter was too strong for her. As he led her out into the snow, she saw that it was already a few feet deep and she could barely see a few centimetres in front of her face.

"I'll ride back," Sarah insisted as she tried to wriggle out of Alex's grasp.

"Don't be ridiculous," Alex said. He picked her up and carried her through the snow to the carriage.

He put her inside and climbed in after her. Pattinson

leapt in and settled himself on the floor.

"I can't leave Black Guy out there in this," Sarah protested as she tried to climb out of the carriage.

"He's already tied to the back of the carriage. I'm not letting you go out in this weather on your own," Alex said as he forced her to sit down.

The carriage lurched forward slowly as the driver tried to peer through the heavy snow. Sarah sat in silence next to Alex. Part of her was glad to see him, but she was still hurt by his departure, and his boorish behaviour dragging her out of the police house had annoyed her.

Mr Hunter knew that her ladyship was angry with him. He didn't have much experience dealing with women, but he knew how to read people.

He thought about trying to talk to her, but her body language told him it wasn't the best idea. The carriage was crawling forward at a pace that was half the speed of a walking man.

It seemed like it had been an eternity that Alex had sat in the carriage beside Sarah. She seemed content to stare out of the window at the falling snow, but the silence became too intense for the young hunter to bear.

"You seem to have recovered well," Alex said. Sarah spun her head and glared at the hunter. Her eyes were filled with hatred and anger. Alex had never thought that he would see Sarah look that way at anyone, least of all him.

She didn't reply to him, she just stared at him. The longer she glared, the more uncomfortable Alex felt. He had hunting creatures that could kill him with a single swipe. He had stood up to men that were cold and heartless killers. But under the unwavering gaze of this lady filled with such rage, he quailed.

"I'm sorry," he said softly.

"For what?" Sarah demanded acidly.

"For dragging you out of the police house," Alex said sheepishly.

"That's not what you should be apologising for," Sarah spat back.

"Then what -" Alex began, but Sarah but him off.

"You left without saying a word. You just went to Scotland. You didn't say you were going; you didn't come to the house when I was recovering. You turned your back on me when I called out to you," Sarah raged. Her eyes were filled with tears, and she turned away from Alex so that he wouldn't see her crying.

Alex sat beside her. He was lost for words. The carriage came to a stop, and the driver opened the door.

"We're here, my lady." the driver said, and Sarah leapt from the carriage as quickly as she could and tried to stride hurriedly through the snowdrift that lay between the carriage and the house.

"Sarah, wait!" Alex called out as he leapt out of the carriage after her.

The sound of Alex calling out caused the door to the house to be thrown open, and Bosworth emerged carrying a lantern.

"My lady, thank goodness. We feared that with the storm you would be stuck in the village," Bosworth said as he helped Sarah into the house.

"Mr Hunter brought me back," Sarah said sharply as she shook the snow from her cloak.

"Mr Hunter? He's back from the north?" Bosworth asked as he turned back towards the carriage and spotted Alex making his way through the snow.

"So it seems," Sarah said dryly and marched across the hall to the staircase.

"My lady, you have some guests waiting for you in the drawing room," Bosworth called after her.

"Who is it?" Sarah asked as she reached the stairs.

"Mr Cooper," Bosworth replied as Alex walked through the door, his dog at his side.

"Sarah, please," Alex begged.

"Give Mr Cooper my apologies. I am feeling unwell," Sarah said and turned away from the two men. She walked up the stairs and slammed the door to her rooms.

Grace's room was not connected to Sarah's, so she knew she was alone. The moment the door had closed, Sarah leant back against the wall and started to cry.

"Hunter! I thought I heard your voice," Daniel said brightly as he stepped into the hall.

"Cooper," Alex said, nodding to his school friend.

"What brings you here?" Daniel asked as he offered the hunter his hand. Pattinson growled slightly, and Daniel quickly withdrew his hand.

"I brought her ladyship back from the village," Alex explained.

"Ah, good, where is she?" Daniel asked, looking around the hall.

"Her ladyship sends her apologies, sir. She is feeling unwell," Bosworth offered.

"Nothing serious, I hope?" Daniel asked with concern.

"She will be fine after she has rested, I'm certain," Bosworth assured him.

"Where is the brigadier?" Alex asked.

"He went to see Doctor Hales early this morning. He is not expected back until later this evening," Bosworth replied.

"I am sure that her ladyship would want you to make her guest comfortable until the storm has passed. I will see to the horses," Alex said as he stepped back into the storm.

"If you would follow me, Mr Cooper," Bosworth asked as he led Daniel back to the drawing room.

Chapter 4

Sarah didn't leave her room until the next morning, when she was certain that Alex and Daniel had both left.

The snow lay in a thick blanket over the Grangeback Estate. It had snowed until late into the evening, when the footmen and gardeners had been put to work clearing the paths and drive. Alex had helped them work whilst Daniel had stood watching their progress.

When he was satisfied his carriage would be able to make it to the road, he had left. Alex had chosen to stay at Grangeback until the brigadier came home.

As Sarah descended to take breakfast in the dining room, she was met by the sight of Alex sat at the dining table.

"What are you doing here?" Sarah frowned.

"I didn't go home last night. I was waiting for the brigadier to come back before I left, but he spent the night at Doctor Hales," Alex explained.

"So you stayed here all night? Where did you sleep?" Sarah asked coldly.

"The floor in the drawing room is quite comfortable," Alex replied without the smallest hint of humour. The atmosphere in the dining room was tense as Sarah helped herself to the contents of the silver serving dishes.

"I'm sorry I hurt you," Alex said after a moment of silence. Sarah stopped spooning food onto her plate and waited for Alex to continue.

"I don't understand why you acted that way," Sarah said when it was clear Alex was waiting for her to respond.

"Your ladyship -" Alex began.

"Don't call me that," Sarah snapped.

"What?" Alex asked as Sarah turned to face him.

"Don't call me 'your ladyship'; I know what you are doing when you say that. I am Sarah, and you are Alex," Sarah half-shouted.

"Your ladyship -" Alex said again.

"Stop it!" Sarah said with tears in her eyes. Alex slowly got up from the dinner table and walked over to where Sarah was standing.

"You know we can't do this. You are woman of prominence. I'm a hunter, a mere groundskeeper," Alex said as he tilted her chin up so that she was looking at him.

"When has that ever mattered to me?" Sarah asked quietly.

"I won't ruin you," Alex replied softly.

"That's why you've been so distant? You're trying to make me hate you?" Sarah asked.

"No, I'm trying to protect myself. I can't keep spending time with you when there are men coming to call on you. Men that want to marry you. Men that can marry you and not leave you open to scandal," Alex explained.

"Breeding doesn't mean there won't be a scandal," Sarah smiled.

Alex opened his mouth to reply as the doors to the dining room were flung open.

"Ah good morning!" George said in a bright voice.

"George," Alex nodded and stepped away from Sarah.

"Bosworth told me you were back, when we've eaten, you'll have to tell me all about your time in the highlands," George said, clapping his hands.

"I'll wait for you in the study," Alex said and left Sarah and the brigadier to their breakfast.

"Did I interrupt something?" George asked as he looked at Sarah.

"Yes, but it may have been for the best," Sarah sighed, "is that the morning paper?" she asked.

"It is, there is an interesting story that you will find especially pertinent," George said as he handed Sarah the newspaper.

"Oh?" Sarah asked as she made her way to the table with her breakfast.

"Miss Moore and Miss Beech, two of the women that kidnapped you, they died a few days ago," George said as he joined Sarah at the table.

"What?" Sarah frowned as she opened the paper and scanned through the columns looking for the story.

"Apparently they both fell ill and died not long after. It's all on page seven," George said and ate his breakfast.

Sarah read through the story detailing the circumstances of their deaths. As she read, she felt her stomach sinking. It was a sickening sensation that left her in no mood to eat.

"What are your plans for the day?" George asked, seemingly unaware of the effect the news was having on Sarah.

"I'll be going down to Stickleback with Grace," Sarah

said as she folded up the newspaper.

"If it starts snowing, make sure to come straight back. Don't want you to get stranded down in the village,." George replied.

"I will," Sarah promised and left the dining room.

George finished eating his breakfast and then made his way to the study.

"Are things as bad as we feared in Scotland?" George asked as he entered. Pattinson was lying by the fire in the library. He had spent the night leaping through snowdrifts, so he was now cold and tired.

"Unless there is a cull, the deer will be starving, there will be no new trees, and in a few hundred years the forests will be gone," Alex sighed as George sat down.

"Did they listen?" the brigadier asked.

"Of course not. None of them live on the estates any more, they are little more than retreats from the cities," Alex said crossly.

"What was going on between you and Sarah in the dining room?" George asked, changing the subject.

"Nothing. Has Mr Cooper made any further advances?" Alex asked.

"None, no one has been to the house since you left," George shrugged.

"He was here last night," Alex raised his eyebrow.

"Was he indeed? Did he see Sarah?" George leaned forwards over his desk.

"No, she was too upset to see anyone," Alex replied.

"She was upset?" George frowned.

"It was my fault," Alex admitted.

"You upset Sarah?" George looked bemused at the idea.

"She didn't like me leaving without saying goodbye – amongst other things," Alex squirmed uncomfortably in his chair.

"Is that so?" George grinned.

"You know that I am not a gentleman. Daniel is," Alex said sharply.

"You have always been too preoccupied with positions in life," George said, shaking his head.

"Society is too preoccupied with them. I am merely practical," Alex insisted.

"But has that practicality ever made you happy, my boy?" George asked gently.

50

"I should be getting back to the lodge," Alex said abruptly. He left the study quickly, leaving George in the study. The brigadier grinned to himself. Life had certainly become a lot more interesting with Sarah in the house.

Grace and Sarah rode down into Stickleback. They kept to the roads as the snow hid all sorts of dangers when riding across the fields. The last thing that Sarah wanted was for Black Guy to break his leg stepping into a rabbit's hole that was hidden by the snow.

Sarah led the way through the village streets, saying good morning to people as she passed. She took the horses to the inn and left them with the stable boys, before leading Grace to the police house.

"Back again?" Arwyn frowned as he opened the door. He wore his new whistle and chain, proudly puffing out his chest so that Sarah could see he was wearing them.

"What happened to Miss Turner?" Sarah asked as she stepped into the police house.

"Miss Turner?" Arwyn looked confused.

"The three women that kidnapped me, Miss Beech, Miss Moore and Miss Turner. What happened to Miss Turner?" Sarah asked.

"She was released on bail to a gentleman. Her solicitor arranged it. No one has seen her since then though. Why?" Arwyn asked worriedly.

"Miss Beech and Miss Moore are dead," Sarah said flatly.

"What? How?" Arwyn asked.

"They died from a fever, one that sounded incredibly similar to the fever that my parents and my household in India died from," Sarah replied.

"I see, well, I will try and find out what happened to Miss Turner, but there isn't much I can do about Miss Moore and Miss Beech," Arwyn shrugged.

"No, of course not," Sarah said and shook her head in frustration.

"Was there anything else?" Arwyn asked.

"Oh, Constable Arwyn Evans, this is Miss Grace Read, she is my lady's maid," Sarah said.

"Pleased to meet you," Grace smiled.

"I am sure you will find working for her ladyship to be quite interesting," Constable Evans said tactfully.

"It's already been quite educational," Grace giggled.

"We should be heading back to the house," Sarah said

and left Arwyn to his duties.

Sarah didn't say much on their ride back to Grangeback, her head was clouded with thoughts. Grace didn't mind riding in silence, though she felt confused by Sarah's demeanour.

Chapter 5

An invitation arrived at Grangeback not long after Sarah and Grace set out for Stickleback. It was addressed to George.

Brigadier General Webb-Kneelingroach

Please do me the honour of dining with me this lunchtime at Duffleton Hall.

Lord Daniel Cooper.

George thought about declining the offer, but decided it would be extremely rude to turn down a handwritten invitation to lunch.

He took one of the smaller carriages and arrived at Duffleton at 12 o'clock.

"My dear brigadier, wonderful to see you. So glad you could come," Daniel said as he shook George's hand.

"It doesn't do to decline a neighbour's luncheon invitation," George replied with some bluster.

"Of course not! Come and meet the rest of our merry band," Daniel beckoned and led George through the house to the billiard room, "May I introduce Lord Joshua St. Vincent, his brother Mr Callum St. Vincent, Mr Jake Walker, Mr Stuart Moore, Mr Samuel Jones, Mr Luke Lumb, Mr Timothy Wood, Mr Richard Ball, Mr Michael Hutton, Mr Joe Blatherwick and Mr Gregory Kitts," Daniel said pointing to each of the gentlemen in turn.

"Good morning," George said warmly.

"Gentlemen, this is Brigadier General George Webb-Kneelingroach from the Grangeback estate. I think you have met Mr Walker and Mr Moore before," Daniel said.

"Yes, they were at the house on All Hallows' Eve," George agreed.

"Excellent, well please, make yourself at home. Lunch will be served in half an hour, then I thought cards would be a grand distraction," Daniel grinned.

"Brigadier, so wonderful to finally meet you, I've heard so much about you," Lord St. Vincent said, extending his hand to George.

"What brings you to England, my lord, the last news from court said you were in the Far East," George asked as he shook the young lord's hand.

"One can only remain in the Orient so long before the longing for dear England becomes too overpowering," Joshua grinned.

"Well that I cannot fault you for. Are you staying here at Duffleton?" George asked.

"Most of the party is. I did have rooms in Chester, but dear Daniel insisted that my brother and I come and enjoy his hospitality. Mr Walker and Mr Moore are here for lunch and the daily distraction of any sport we can find. I believe that Mr Thomas and Edward Egerton are also due to join us for lunch," Joshua explained.

"Ah, is there much sport to be had on the estate?" George inquired.

"No, not so far. Daniel has kept us entertained with billiards and cards, but there seems to be little in the way of shooting and fishing here," Joshua sighed.

"Well that is something we must remedy. There is plenty of sport to be had on the Grangeback estate; you must all come to the house for a few weeks. I will have my hunt master take you hunting and fishing. I daresay that you could all use the distraction," George said grandly.

"A splendid idea, and yet another change of scenery. You forget how excellent the hospitality of English houses is when you are away for so long," Joshua smiled warmly.

"Did I just hear an invitation being offer?" Mr Lumb asked as he joined Joshua and George.

"My dear Luke, the brigadier has kindly invited us all to Grangeback to enjoy shooting and fishing under the instruction of his hunt master," Joshua said clapping a hand on Mr Lumb's shoulder.

"What a capital idea! Old Hunter is your hunt master is he not?" Luke asked eagerly.

"He is, you went to school with him?" George asked.

"Why of course we did, I think only Lord and Mr St. Vincent are the only ones here who don't know Old Hunter," Luke said clapping his hands together with delight.

"What was that about Old Hunter?" Mr Blatherwick asked, calling from the other side of the room.

"He's the hunt master at Grangeback. The brigadier's invited us to stay and have Old Hunter take us shooting and fishing," Luke shouted back. The room broke out into a chorus of cheers and laughter at the idea, the topics of conversation turning to what a good time they would all have staying on the brigadier's estate.

As George listened to the conversations, he began to get an uneasy feeling. It had seemed like such a good idea to invite the young men to stay, but the longer he thought about it, the more he was sure that it was going to bring nothing but trouble.

"Lord Cooper, Mr Thomas Egerton and Mr Edward Egerton have arrived," the butler announced from the doorway.

"Excellent, everyone is here; well shall we adjourn to the dining room? We can hash out a plan for this splendid shooting and fishing and then enjoy brandy, port and bridge," Daniel called over the general noise in the room.

"I have a suspicion that you play a rather fine hand of cards," Joshua said to George as the party moved from the billiard room to the dining room.

"I think you are probably a better card player than I. It's been years since I played properly," George replied.

"Then, as the finest card players in the room, I think we should partner in this grand bridge tournament that Lord

Cooper is inflicting on us," Joshua grinned.

"If we're the finest players in the room, won't that make it rather dull play?" George asked.

"Of course not, we can set challenges for each hand, see by just how much we can outplay our opponents. I think you'd be a worthy ally in such an endeavour," Joshua grinned.

"I will admit, it does sound more appealing than partnering with Lord Cooper. He is known to be a terrible player," George allowed.

"Then it is settled. We shall take all before us and celebrate this evening at Grangeback," Lord St. Vincent said as lunch was served.

It was decided that rather than stay at Grangeback, the gentlemen who were already staying at Duffleton would travel back each night. Mr Walker, Mr Moore and both Mr Egertons would trespass upon the hospitality of Grangeback.

George insisted that the party join him for dinner each evening after the day's sport was done.

It was generally agreed that this was the best plan. George and Joshua won the bridge tournament bringing an end to the afternoon at Duffleton.

On his way back to Grangeback, George called in to tell

Alex about the shooting and fishing so that he could make preparations for the following day.

There was a flicker of irritation that passed over Alex's face when George told him who the party consisted of, but he agreed to be ready in the morning.

As George left Alex sat down beside the fire.

"Lord and Mr St. Vincent at Grangeback with Sarah, sounds like a recipe for disaster to me," Mr Hunter said as he stroked Pattinson's head.

Chapter 6

Mr Hunter made sure that he was at Grangeback bright and early the next day. He thought it was best if he intercepted the hunting party before Lord St. Vincent and Mr St. Vincent could interact with Lady Sarah.

Pattinson knew that something different was happening. Their normal routine of working in the grounds and hunting in the woods didn't involve visiting the main house with a large number of shotguns.

Alex had also been down into the village before he went to Grangeback to hire Stanley and Lee Baker to help with the hunt. The two boys were paid to carry guns, ammunition, fishing rods, bait, the birds that were shot and the fish that were caught.

He had warned the boys that they were to wait behind the men whilst they were firing and wait for Alex's instruction before collecting the birds. They spent an hour preparing the equipment outside the main house before the party of gentlemen arrived.

Mr Walker, Mr Moore, and both Mr Egertons arrived with their belongings, and the footmen carried them into the rooms that George had Mrs Bosworth prepared for the four men.

The others arrived on horseback. Whilst the majority of the party took their horses to the stable, Daniel took the opportunity to try and call on Lady Sarah.

"Good morning, Bosworth, is her ladyship awake yet?" Daniel asked.

"I'm afraid not, my lord," Bosworth replied.

"Then can you pass on my regards to her ladyship?" Daniel said, looking towards the stair, hoping for a glimpse of Sarah descending for breakfast.

"I will have Miss Grace pass on the message,." Bosworth agreed.

"Miss Grace?" Daniel furrowed his brow.

"Her ladyship's lady's maid," Bosworth replied.

"Ah excellent, thank you, Bosworth," Daniel said cheerfully.

"You are welcome, my lord. A good day hunting to you," Bosworth bowed slightly and went about his duties.

Alex was greeted with a large measure of gusto by his

old school friends. They were all far more excited about seeing him than he was at seeing them. Mr Hunter didn't remember his school days fondly. He was the son of a lady's maid. His mother had died in an accident that had also deprived the brigadier of his wife.

Alex had only been a young boy at the time. He had never known who his father was or met him as far as he knew. George had taken responsibility for raising the boy and sent him to school.

Because he wasn't the son of a gentleman, he was bullied and treated badly by the men that now greeted him so warmly. It had taken Alex saving a handful of them from a dangerous situation in Chester to earn their respect and friendship – neither of which had he ever sought.

As Daniel joined the party, the guns were passed out, and Alex led the group into the forests so they could reach the land beyond the trees that led to the grounds where they would be shooting pheasant and partridge amongst other game birds.

Pattinson bounded around Alex's legs as they walked to the trees, he had never been part of a shooting party before, and the large number of men walking with them had excited the dog. The paws of the dog sent snow spraying over the men as he leapt about.

Sarah stood at her window and watched the men walking towards the wood. A smile spread across her lips at the sight of Pattinson. The dog had belonged to the women that had kidnapped Sarah. The dog had once attacked Alex and left him near death, but in their second encounter, Pattinson had been shot.

Rather than leaving the dog for dead, Alex had taken the injured animal home and nursed it back to health. Since then, Pattinson hadn't left Alex's side.

"Good morning, my lady. Mr Daniel Cooper sends his compliments," Grace said as she entered the room.

"Thank you, Grace," Sarah said with a sigh.

"He's a fine man, my lady," Grace said with approval.

"He's a young man, whether he is fine, I don't know yet. Has there been any message from Constable Evans?" Sarah asked.

"No, my lady," Grace said as she laid out Sarah's clothes for the day.

"Then we will go and visit him," Sarah said firmly.

"As you wish, my lady. I will have the horses

prepared," Grace replied and left the room.

The lady's maid walked down the servants stairs to the kitchen. She used the back door to reach the stables. When she had given the instruction to the grooms, she returned to the house.

She was still treated as an outsider by most of the household staff. A lot of them had lived in Grangeback for most of their lives, serving the family in one capacity or another. Mrs Bosworth was nice enough, as was Cooky, but the rest of the staff were cold and distant.

Grace also had the feeling that there were a lot of things that she didn't know; that there were family secrets that were being jealously guarded by the servants.

Sarah's preoccupation with the women she had mentioned to the constable concerned Grace. She had a horrible feeling that there was much more going on than simple curiosity over the fate of three criminals.

Grace had read about the kidnapping and the arrest of the three women in the paper. She knew that Sarah had been gravely injured and that Lord Daniel Cooper had been credited with her rescue.

It had been the talk of Chester until the scandal

involving her former master. She had no doubt that the gentlemen that were visiting Lord Cooper and had come to shoot on the Grangeback estate had all come to see the heroic lord and his damsel-in-distress.

That they would be able to return home at the end of the visit and provide their social circles with further gossip that would keep talk of the kidnapping alive for months.

Yet, from all that Grace had heard, Sarah was not the damsel-in-distress that the stories painted, and from what she had been told of Lord Cooper, he was not the heroic figure either.

As she walked back to the kitchen, she resolved to discover the truth behind the gossip. Cooky was alone in the kitchen when Grace came back in, so Grace took the opportunity to question her.

"Cooky, can you tell me what really happened on All Hallows' Eve?" Grace's hands twitched nervously as she spoke.

"Have you not heard the stories already?" Cooky asked.

"I don't want to hear the stories; I want to know the truth," Grace said firmly.

"Then you are not alone. There are only four people who know what happened that night and only one of them has spoken of it," Cooky said, shaking her head.

"Who was there? Who told the story?" Grace pressed.

"Lady Sarah, Lord Cooper, Constable Evans and Mr Hunter were the ones that were there, if you don't include that beast of a dog. Only Lord Cooper has spoken about that night to anyone," Cooky replied.

"So all the stories of what happened are what Lord Cooper has told people?" Grace asked.

"Of course," Cooky smiled.

"I see. Thank you," Grace said and returned to Sarah's room.

Sarah had dressed without help and appeared to be ready to ride into Stickleback. The clothes that Grace had laid out for Sarah were almost identical to the clothes that the lady's maid wore.

They had been made by Miss Baker to accommodate Sarah's wilder approach to life. Grace still felt uncomfortable wearing them, but they were far more practical than the dresses she was used to wearing.

As the two women rode down into Stickleback, they

could hear the sound of guns being fired in the distance.

It grew fainter as they entered the village, and by the time they reached the inn, the sound was little more than a distant ringing.

They left the horses at the inn, as they had the day before, and went to call on Constable Evans.

"My lady, there is really nothing I can tell you," Arwyn said with a sigh as he found Sarah at his door.

"I don't believe you," Sarah said and swept past the constable.

"Lady Sarah, I know that you are upset about this, but -" Arwyn began, but Sarah cut across him.

"I am going to find out how Miss Beech and Miss Moore died. I am going to find out where Miss Turner is. I am going to find out who was behind the events on All Hallows' Eve. You can help me, or you can tell me to be on my way," Sarah said in a no-nonsense voice.

Arwyn looked at Sarah and shook his head.

"Fine," he sighed, "but you will let me do things properly, following procedures and guidelines. I don't want to have the Chief Constable turning up at my door again. I am already close to losing my job as it is," he told Sarah firmly.

"You'll never lose your job, Arwyn, I won't allow it," Sarah smiled at the constable.

Grace didn't say a word as Arwyn and Sarah sat down and discussed their plans. She had never heard anyone talk about things like this before. She was fascinated, scared and oddly excited.

Chapter 7

Sarah didn't mention to anyone that she was looking into the deaths of Miss Beech and Miss Moore. With Mr Moore staying at Grangeback for the duration of the shooting, it seemed rather more tactful to keep it to herself.

Every night the men came to dinner at Grangeback, and the table was full of game and fish that had been brought back by the men.

Sarah was expected to play the part of the charming hostess, which she did for George's sake without complaint.

Seeing Thomas and Edward Egerton again after the excitement on All Hallows' Eve had been rather awkward at first, but after an hour of talking, they were once again at ease with each other.

Daniel was attentive to Sarah at every possible opportunity, sitting beside her at dinner and trying to dominate every conversation with her.

Alex had been included in the dinner party, his time

being monopolised by his old school friends, but he never stopped watching what Lord Joshua St. Vincent and Mr Callum St. Vincent were doing. But, despite his misgivings at having them both at Grangeback and close to Sarah, nothing happened.

Alex began to relax and even enjoyed spending time with the men that had once made him miserable.

On the fifth day of the shooting party, a telegram was brought during dinner and handed to Sarah. It had been delivered without an envelope and in order to discover who it was for, Sarah had to read it.

It feels like an eternity since we last met. My world is cold and without light in your absence. Are you ever going to return to me, Mr Hunter?

Yours evermore

Heather

As Sarah read the words on the page, she felt her stomach fall. It was as though she had been plunged into an

71

icy river and left to drown.

The pain she felt at reading the telegram only registered in the briefest of flickers across her face before she placed a mask of smiles to cover it.

"It is for Mr Hunter," Sarah told Bosworth, who delivered the telegram down the table to where Alex sat.

Sarah watched Alex out of the corner of his eye as he opened and read the message. He exchanged a few words with Bosworth before he stood from the table and walked over to the fire.

The telegram was crumpled in his hand and he threw the paper onto the flames in the grate. Alex glanced over at Sarah, but she seemed to be engaged in conversation with Daniel, paying no attention whatsoever to the hunter.

Alex took a deep breath and returned to the table. Sarah made no effort to speak to Alex about the telegram and he had no intention of discussing its contents if he didn't have to.

The telegram had been brought from the village by Constable Evans, along with a message for Sarah. As they were engaged in dinner, Bosworth had taken the constable to Grace to leave the message with her.

Grace had been surprised to see the constable at the house so late in the day, but she also saw an opportunity.

"Good evening, constable, can I offer you some tea?" Grace asked as Arwyn was shown into the kitchen.

"Thank you, it is bitter out," Arwyn replied as he sat down at the table, opposite Grace.

The lady's maid filled the kettle with water and set it to boiling over the fire.

"I wanted to ask you something," Grace said slowly as she sat down again

"Oh?" Arwyn hadn't been expecting any conversation from the lady's maid.

"You were there on All Hallows' Eve. I've heard the stories, but I don't believe them. Can you tell me what really happened?" Grace blurted out, her face turning red.

"Why don't you believe the stories?" Arwyn asked with a wry smile playing on his lips.

"Because my lady isn't a damsel-in-distress, and Lord Cooper is no different from any other young man in society that I have encountered," Grace explained.

"Those are good reasons, very well, but you cannot repeat anything I tell you to anyone else," Arwyn said sternly.

"Agreed," Grace smiled.

"I assume you know that Mr Cooper disappeared along with Mr Taylor, that Lady Sarah found Mr Hunter half-dead in the woods. All of that is true. I suspect that what you want to know about is what happened on the Edge." Arwyn said, and Grace nodded.

"It was rather confusing, but Sarah had been shot. She was tied up, and there was nothing she could do. I don't think she was conscious during any part of what happened. The stories tell of Lord Cooper rushing in, killing the dogs and carrying Sarah to safety," Arwyn sighed.

"But that didn't happen?" Grace asked.

"No, all Lord Cooper did was injure Pattinson. It was Mr Hunter who followed the trail that led us to Lady Sarah. He shot Miss Turner in the shoulder with an arrow despite being weak and having an injured shoulder. I killed the other two dogs, but it was Mr Hunter that saved Lady Sarah," Arwyn said.

"Lady Sarah doesn't know?" Grace gasped.

"No, Mr Hunter won't have told her, and he swore me to secrecy on the subject," Arwyn shrugged as Grace went to attend to the boiling kettle.

"But surely she should know who really saved her life," Grace insisted as she poured the hot water into the teapot.

"No, she shouldn't."

Grace and Arwyn both turned to see Alex stood in the kitchen doorway.

"How can you say that, Mr Hunter?" Grace asked in disbelief.

"Because it is better that Lord Cooper has the credit," Alex said firmly.

"Aren't you supposed to be enjoying dinner?" Arwyn asked Alex.

"Bosworth said you brought the telegram for me and that you had a message for Sarah," Alex replied.

"So you wanted to find out what she is getting herself mixed up in?" Arwyn asked.

"Something like that," Alex shrugged as he sat down next to Arwyn.

"She just asked me to look into what killed Miss Beech and Miss Moore. She thought it sounded a lot like the fever that her parents and her household in India died from," Arwyn replied.

"And what did you find out?" Alex asked.

"They were slowly poisoned, but it wasn't anything exotic," Arwyn said.

"Then what was it?" Sarah asked.

"Why aren't you at the dinner table?" Alex demanded.

"Because I saw you leave and you didn't come back," Sarah said shortly.

"Blood poisoning. They both had septicaemia that developed into sepsis according to Doctor Hales," Arwyn said.

"I don't understand." Grace frowned.

"They had an infection that poisoned their blood. Their bodies responded to the infection, but the response caused organ failure, which killed them," Alex explained.

"You know someone who died from sepsis?" Sarah asked.

"Old Mitchell. He cut his hand on a piece of metal. It got infected, and by the time we got him to Doctor Hales there was nothing he could do," Alex explained.

"It can be caused by a cut?" Grace asked in a slightly panicked voice.

"A cut, a dirty needle, an old burn that never healed properly," Sarah said as she leaned against the wall, "There were lots of people in India who died from it."

"So it wasn't the same thing that killed your family?" Arwyn asked.

"I don't know, but it is still suspicious that both of them contracted blood poisoning and died, and then Miss Turner disappears. I need to talk to the brigadier," Sarah replied.

"We should return to the dining room. This will keep until tomorrow," Alex said, and steered Sarah out of the kitchen.

"He called her Sarah," Grace said as soon as Alex and Sarah were out of earshot.

"What?" Arwyn frowned.

"He didn't call her my lady, your ladyship or Lady Sarah. He called her Sarah. He's in love with her," Grace replied.

"He is," Arwyn agreed.

"But he's just a hunter. He can't possibly think that they can be together," Grace frowned.

"He doesn't. But it doesn't change how much he loves her," Arwyn sighed.

Chapter 8

Lady Szonja, the Countess of Huntingdon was a woman of no small refinement. She embodied the ideals of grace and style that most women within society aspired to.

Yet she was not a foolish woman. She had lived long enough to gather wisdom and was as wary of young men around young women as the brigadier was.

There had only been one man that the countess had ever loved. He had been a prince of Hungary and had died in the city of Pest when it had flooded earlier in the year.

She had been heartbroken ever since, but it didn't show in her public countenance. She reserved her grief from when she was alone and could lament the loss of her love.

She was the cousin of Mrs Egerton of Tatton Park and had been visiting her for several months. The countess had been there on All Hallows' Eve and had found Sarah to be quite charming.

Despite this, it was a surprise to Sarah when the

countess arrived at Grangeback completely unannounced.

It was the day after Arwyn had brought news of the blood poisoning to Sarah. Sarah was eating breakfast when the countess was shown in.

"Lady Szonja, what a pleasant surprise," Sarah said as she dropped her cutlery.

"Forgive me for not calling on you sooner," the countess replied.

"Have you had breakfast?" Sarah asked as she stood up from the table.

"I have, I didn't mean to interrupt yours, but there is something that is most urgent that I need to discuss with you," Lady Szonja frowned.

"Of course, we can talk in the drawing room," Sarah said worriedly and led the countess through the house.

"My nephews are staying as part of the shooting party, is that correct?" the countess asked as she sat down.

"It is, I have only seen them at dinner though, they spend the day out shooting and fishing," Sarah said slowly.

"And the shooting party has many gentlemen as part of it. Are they all staying here at Grangeback?" Lady Sonja continued.

"No, your nephews, Mr Moore and Mr Walker are the only gentlemen that are staying at the house," Sarah replied, her confusion growing.

"That is something at least. There are two of the gentlemen that are part of the party that I must warn you about. They are not men to be trusted," Lady Szonja said sternly.

"Who are they?" Sarah asked.

"Lord Joshua St. Vincent and Mr Callum St. Vincent. They are men that are well thought of by society, but they are men left wanting as far as good character is concerned," the countess said firmly.

"They are part of the party, but they haven't spoken a word to me in all their time here. I met Lord St. Vincent in Chester not long ago, but that is the only time either of them has ever spoken to me," Sarah assured the countess.

"Then let my warning serve you well," Lady Szonja sighed with relief.

"Why do you think that they are men of poor character?" Sarah asked.

"There is nothing I can tell you with any certainty, only that there is something about them that I do not trust," the countess said seriously.

"Then I will be cautious," Sarah replied.

"Good, now I will leave you to finish your breakfast," Lady Szonja smiled and left the drawing room without waiting for Sarah to say goodbye.

Sarah sat in the drawing room for a few minutes and thought about the countess had said. She hadn't liked Lord St. Vincent when she had met him in Chester and Grace had warned her then to avoid the young lord.

"Ah, Sarah, there you are!" the brigadier said brightly, interrupting her thoughts, "You left your breakfast half-finished, is everything all right?" he asked as he sat down next to Sarah.

"The two women that died in jail; Miss Beech and Miss Moore, they were both poisoned," Sarah said slowly.

"Are you sure?" the brigadier asked.

"Yes, Constable Evans had Doctor Hales look into it for me. It was too suspicious that they both died not long after being arrested. Miss Turner has also disappeared after she was released into the care of a gentleman," Sarah continued.

"You think all of this is connected?" the brigadier asked.

"I think it has something to do with my parents dying. It is too much of a coincidence," Sarah said, shaking her head.

"I'm sure it is nothing to worry about," the brigadier said patting Sarah's arm comfortingly, "Now come, shake off these worries. I am going down to visit Doctor Hales to invite him to dine with all of us this evening. I shouldn't be too long," George smiled and left Sarah in the drawing room.

His carriage was already waiting for him as he stepped out of the front door. It was a short journey from Grangeback to Doctor Hales' house in the village, but it was long enough for George to think over what he would do about Sarah.

Doctor Hales accepted the invitation for dinner, and George left to return to Stickleback, but instead of going directly to the house, he told the driver to take him to the police house.

The carriage pulled up outside the small building, and Arwyn opened the door. He had been expecting the brigadier to call after what Sarah had said the night before.

Constable Evans welcomed the brigadier into the police house and waited patiently for George to tell him what he was there for.

"Arwyn, you've been a very good constable for this

village, and you did extremely well to find Sarah on All Hallows' Eve," George said as he sat down.

"Thank you, brigadier, it's most kind of you to say so," Arwyn replied.

"I've never had any cause to be displeased with your work, until now," George said seriously.

"You want me to stop investigating the disappearance of Miss Turner," Arwyn sighed heavily.

"I want you to stop helping Sarah. The more she digs into all of this, the more danger she will be in. I can't have her put in any further danger. I have lost one daughter already; I don't need to lose another," George replied with lips set in a thin line.

"If that's what you want, sir, but she won't stop trying to find out what happened. She's a tenacious woman," Arwyn replied.

"I know, but without your help it should make it much harder for her to find anything out and those that are hunting her will see her as less of a threat," George said as he rubbed his eyes.

"We can only hope so. What will you tell her ladyship?" Constable Evans asked.

"I don't know. Does Mr Hunter know about this?" George asked.

"Yes, he was there last night when I told her ladyship what Doctor Hales had found," Arwyn replied.

"Very well, thank you, constable," George said, holding out his hand to the policeman. Arwyn shook the brigadier's hand and watched him leave. The constable felt relieved as George left and wondered how on Earth the brigadier was going to convince Sarah to stop her own enquiries.

As the carriage arrived back at Grangeback, George didn't go into the house; instead, he set off to find the shooting party. It wasn't difficult to discover where they were; the firing guns made it fairly easy to find them.

The brigadier stood behind Stanley and Lee Baker as the men fired at the birds that Pattinson was flushing out.

"Things seem to be going well," George smiled as Alex came out of the hide that he was shooting from.

"There will be plenty of food on the table tonight," Mr Hunter grinned, "What brings you out here?" he asked.

"I needed to talk with you. Walk with me for a while. I am sure the party will be fine without you for a few minutes," the brigadier said as he led Alex away from the sound of the guns.

"What's wrong?" Alex frowned as the two men were far enough away to not need to shout to be heard.

"Sarah spoke to me this morning. She mentioned that Constable Evans told her that Miss Beech and Miss Moore were poisoned," the brigadier said in a low voice.

"Sepsis caused by septicaemia," Alex nodded.

"I've told him to stop helping her investigate. It's too dangerous. Those women were killed for failing. Miss Turner has disappeared. It's not a coincidence. I will not lose Sarah to this," the brigadier said sharply.

"What do you want me to do?" Alex asked.

"Talk to her. Stop her from digging into this mess," George said earnestly.

"She won't listen," Alex warned.

"Do whatever you can. Constable Evans won't help her any further," the brigadier said and clapped his hand onto Alex's shoulder.

"I'll talk to her tonight," Alex sighed.

Alex was true to his word. After dinner had been finished and most of the party was returning to Duffleton Hall, Mr Hunter took Sarah to one side to talk to her.

"What do you want?" Sarah asked as Alex half-dragged her into the study and shut the door.

"I don't think that Miss Beech and Miss Moore dying had anything to do with what happened to your parents. I think Miss Turner has run away to avoid going to jail," Alex said firmly.

"And what has led you to that conclusion?" Sarah asked, narrowing her eyes.

"You have tunnel vision because you see similarities between what happened with them and what happened to your parents," Alex replied.

"I was kidnapped by three women who questioned me about poppies and shot me! It must have something to do with my parents," Sarah spat back.

"Or it could be that any one of the people you have met since coming to England are involved in the opium trade to China, and these women were working for the Chinese government," Alex said flatly.

"What do you know about the opium trade in China?" Sarah asked acidly.

"Enough to know that anyone who is in trade and has interests in the East India Company could be involved," Mr

Hunter said, giving Sarah a withering look.

"So you expect me to listen to you and just agree with your conclusions?" Sarah asked.

"I expect you to exercise some sense and use your God-given brain," Alex raised his voice.

"No, you expect me to do as I'm told," Sarah sneered.

"Your ladyship -" Alex said each word slowly as he struggled to control his rising anger.

"I told you not to call me that," Sarah warned.

"Your ladyship, you are making a fool of yourself," Alex was shaking as he spoke.

"I am making a fool of myself?" Sarah asked with incredulity.

"Yes," Alex shot back.

"No. No, you are the one making a fool of yourself. You told me that you are just a groundskeeper, but you talk to me like we're equal. By your logic, we aren't. If we aren't equal enough for you to – if we are not equal, then you have no right to talk to me about any of this," Sarah shouted.

"So you admit that we aren't equal?" Alex asked with a pained expression on his face.

"You have made it clear we are not," Sarah stared at

Alex with a severe glare.

"Then I will bid you goodnight, my lady. I will never trespass on your time again," Alex said and bowed to Sarah. He turned to the door and opened it.

"Go back to Scotland. Go back to your woman there. You are not welcome here," Sarah said as tears rolled down her cheeks.

"As you wish," Alex said, without looking back.

Chapter 9

As the sun rose the next morning, Sarah took Grace down to the lodge. She wanted to call upon Alex and apologise for her behaviour the night before.

It was an hour before the men were due to arrive to shoot. Sarah didn't feel comfortable with just walking into the lodge, so she walked up to the door and raised her hand to knock.

Sarah felt oddly uneasy as she rapped on the door. She waited for an answer or any sign of life to come from within, but there was nothing. She realised that Pattinson wasn't barking at the door.

She tried the handle and found it was locked.

"What's the matter?" Grace asked as Sarah ran around the side of the house to the back door and tried to open it. It was locked as well.

"Mr Hunter never locks his doors," Sarah said worriedly.

She raced back to Grangeback through the woods that surrounded the lodge. Instead of going to the front door, she made for the stables and found that Harald was missing.

"Where is Mr Hunter's horse?" Sarah panted at one of the stable boys.

"Gone, my lady. Mr Hunter came and took him early this morning. He said he was going away. He didn't know when or if he was coming back," the stable boy replied.

There had only been one moment in Sarah's life when she felt like she was going to faint before now. That had been when she had been told of the deaths of her family.

The moment she realised that Alex had left as she had told him to, she felt her legs threaten to collapse, and her head swam with dizziness.

Grace caught Sarah by the waist and helped her to the house. She set the lady down in the kitchen, amidst the early morning bustle of the maids and the footmen.

"What's wrong?" Cooky clucked as Grace sat Sarah down.

"Mr Hunter has gone away," Grace said quietly as she set about making tea for Sarah. Cooky turned pale and rushed out of the kitchen.

"Mrs Bosworth, what is this nonsense, Mr Hunter has left?" Cooky asked as she found Mrs Bosworth in the dining room.

"What are you talking about, Cooky?" Mrs Bosworth asked with a bemused expression on her face.

"Mr Hunter has gone," Cooky said. Mrs Bosworth shook her head.

"Come now, Cooky, he wouldn't just leave. The brigadier will know what is going on," Mrs Bosworth said in a no-nonsense voice and went in search of the brigadier.

She found him sat behind his desk in the study, looking very concerned.

"So it's true, Mr Hunter has gone?" Mrs Bosworth asked quietly when she saw the brigadier's face.

"It is. He left early this morning," the brigadier sighed.

"Did he say why?" Mrs Bosworth asked.

"He said it was better that he go away for a while. That this wasn't where he belonged," George said sadly.

"Brigadier, did you tell him?" Mrs Bosworth asked.

"No, I was tempted to, but he wasn't in a good state when he came to say he was leaving. It wasn't the right time," George replied with a slight shake of his head.

"But he's your son. He needs to know that. This will always be his home," Mrs Bosworth looked distraught at the prospect of Alex's departure.

"He's a grown man. He can make his own decisions," George said as his head fell into his hands.

"He has always been a gentleman playing at being a common man. He just doesn't know it, send someone after him. Bring him back and tell him," Mrs Bosworth begged.

"It will do no good," George said helplessly.

"Then what can we do?" Mrs Bosworth asked.

"We wait for him to come home when he is ready," the brigadier shrugged.

"Sir, I am sorry to interrupt," Bosworth spoke from the door.

"What is it, Bosworth?" George asked, looking up at the butler.

"Lord Daniel Cooper is here. He wishes to speak to you," Bosworth said.

"Very well, show him in," the brigadier said in a weary voice.

"Good morning, brigadier. I got your message about having to cancel the sport. Is everything all right?" Daniel asked as he came in and sat down opposite George.

"My apologies, Mr Hunter was called away," George said shortly.

"Shame, was rather enjoying shooting with Old Hunter. Can't be helped, I suppose," Daniel said as he leaned back in the chair.

"Is there something else?" the brigadier asked when Daniel made no sign of leaving.

"Well, I have been debating when the best time to ask you this would be, but it seems now would be as good a time as any. I am here to ask for your permission to marry your ward," Daniel said in a lazy voice.

It struck George as odd that the young lord would approach the subject in such a relaxed manner.

"Before you can ask for my permission, you will need to discover whether you need royal permission," George frowned.

"Royal permission?" Daniel sat upright in his seat.

"Her Majesty, Queen Victoria, may have to give you permission to wed her ladyship. Her family has an impressive pedigree. If even one member that has contributed to her blood has the blood of George II in their veins, then you will need royal permission," George said seriously.

"I see, then I shall get to it. Good day, brigadier," Daniel said as he stood and left the room.

George sighed with relief. The idea of Sarah marrying Daniel was not one that he found particularly agreeable. In sending him on a wild goose chase to examine Sarah's lineage, he hoped that he had bought enough time for a more suitable suitor to present himself.

Sarah was taken to bed after the shock of Alex's departure. The whole household had become more subdued by the news.

Her ladyship spent two days in her bed staring at the ceiling and questioning why she had been so cruel to the young man and why he had gone.

On the third day, Grace insisted that she get out of bed.

Sarah refused at first, but the more she thought about it, the more she knew that Grace was right. Sarah still had to discover what had happened to Miss Turner.

The young lady assumed that if Alex had come to the conclusion that there was nothing to the disappearance, then Arwyn would be of no help to her.

"We shall go to Chester and see what we can discover

of what happened to Miss Turner," Sarah said firmly. She was determined to prove Mr Hunter wrong. When she did, she would go to Scotland and tell him so.

Chapter 10

For three days Sarah and Grace travelled to Chester. They visited different inns, taverns, hotels, public houses and market stalls, but no one had seen hide nor hair of Miss Turner.

Every evening they returned to Grangeback, Sarah feeling more frustrated and defeated with each failed visit.

After the third day of finding nothing, the young lady sent Grace to talk to Constable Evans. Sarah doubted that anything she said to Arwyn would make the smallest difference, but Grace beseeching him to help on her behalf might yield a better result.

Grace waited until the following morning before she set out for Stickleback Hollow. One of the footmen went with her as an escort to make sure that she didn't get lost on the way to or from the village.

Sarah waited at Grangeback for her to return. It was the servants' afternoon off, so after lunch, Sarah was left alone in the great house.

The brigadier had gone to Manchester for a reunion with some of the men that had served with him in his more glorious campaigns. So Sarah sat in the parlour and sighed every few minutes.

She hadn't realised just how big or empty Grangeback was before now. When she had first arrived, she had wondered how she would manage to feel at home in such a grand and big place.

It hadn't taken very long for her to settle. Part of the reason for that had been Mr Hunter. She was surprised at how lonely she felt, knowing that he wasn't somewhere on the grounds.

Her thoughts about the young hunter were soon interrupted by the arrival of a messenger. As Sarah was the only one in the house, she had to answer the door. A young messenger boy handed over a folded note that was addressed to Sarah and then ran off down the drive without waiting to be paid or for Sarah to say anything.

It seemed very odd to the young lady. She was still mulling over the strange behaviour of the boy as she opened the note.

Your ladyship

I am told that you are trying to discover what happened to my fiancée, Miss Annabel Turner. I think I can be of some assistance.

Meet me on Church Street in Chester at 4 o'clock, and I will be glad to share all that I know.

Yours in sincerity

Lord J. St. Vincent.

Sarah read the note twice and looked at the grandfather clock in the hall. It was already half-past one. In order to reach Chester and meet Lord St. Vincent at the appointed hour, she would have to leave straight away.

Grace had not returned, and there was no one in the house to leave a message with.

"Oh, I'm sorry milady, I didn't realise there was anyone in the house." one of the maids squeaked as she walked into the hall.

"Rosie, I'm glad you are here. When Grace or the brigadier return can you give them this note please? I am going to Chester. Everything they need to know is in there." Sarah said as she pressed the note into the young maid's hands and rushed to gather her belongings before heading for the stable.

Rosie waited for Sarah to disappear out of sight before slipping into the dining room and throwing the note onto the fire that was lit.

Sarah rode Black Guy into the city. She left him at one of the more reputable inns that she had come to know well since arriving from India.

She arrived in the city at half-past three. She had cut across as many of the fields as she could and pushed Black Guy as much as she dared.

Sarah was impressed by how quickly she had reached the city. She was certain that Grace or the brigadier would have returned to the house by now and that Rosie would have passed on the message to one of them.

She arrived at Church Street with ten minutes to spare. She could see that Lord St. Vincent was already waiting for her. He wasn't a man that easily went unnoticed it seemed.

He smiled when he saw Sarah and bowed to her.

"Good afternoon, my lady," he said in a smooth voice.

"You have some information about Miss Turner?" Sarah asked without trading pleasantries with the man.

There was something about him that she didn't like; something in his mannerisms made her feel uncomfortable in his presence. This, coupled with the warnings from Grace and Lady Szonja, were enough to make Sarah want to make this particular meeting as brief as possible.

"I do, walk with me and I shall reveal all," the young lord grinned at Sarah and offered her his arm.

Sarah paused for a moment to think before she accepted the offered arm and allowed Joshua to walk.

"Where are we going?" Sarah asked as Lord St. Vincent escorted her down the street to a carriage and insisted that she board.

"I am taking you to Miss Turner. She is in a hospital in Bache. I am sure she will be very glad of a visit," Joshua replied as he pushed Sarah into the carriage and followed quickly after her.

The carriage lurched forward and trundled out of the city. It was already dark, so no one had seen Sarah being pushed into the carriage on the dimly lit street. No one paid any attention to the carriage as it made its way from the city and out to Bache Hall.

Eventually, the carriage came to a halt outside a grand looking building. Standing outside was a woman with three large looking men.

"What is this place?" Sarah frowned as the woman opened the carriage door.

"Good evening, my lord. Is this the young lady?" the woman said.

"Good evening, Mrs Bird. It is indeed," Joshua smiled nastily at Sarah.

"What's going on?" Sarah demanded.

"Quiet now, girl. Take her inside," the matron ordered the three large men.

"No! What do you think you are doing! Get your hands off me!" Sarah screamed as she tried to push the men back from the carriage door.

Lord St. Vincent watched the altercation for a few moments with amusement before he intervened. He grabbed Sarah by the hair and pulled back her head so he could whisper in her ear.

"This is the Cheshire County Lunatic Asylum. I'm sorry that things ended in this fashion, but my employer needs you out of the way, and a piece of their property returned. You understand. I was hoping that you would be a much more amenable prospect; it would have been so much more enjoyable to see you join with us than this alternative. But it can't be helped. Such devotion to a mere groundskeeper is not a desirable trait for my line of work; so you see, this was really all that I could do – short of killing you of course," Joshua hissed in her ear before he pushed her forcefully out of the carriage and into the waiting arms of the three men.

"Thank you, my lord. We'll see she gets the very best of care," Mrs Bird said with a curtesy.

"I appreciate your help and your discretion, Mrs Bird. You understand the embarrassment, this is my sister," Lord St. Vincent said with a feigned pained expression on his face.

"Of course, my lord, I quite understand. She is listed as Miss Stephanie Hunter in our records to avoid any possible scandal," Mrs Bird replied as Sarah was carried into the hospital, engaged in a futile struggle to escape her captors.

"Thank you, my family will be sure to show it's appreciation for your discretion. If you'll excuse me, I must return to the city, I have a dinner engagement," Lord St. Vincent said, and his carriage lurched away from the hospital leaving Sarah in the hands of the asylum.

Chapter 11

Brigadier George Webb-Kneelingroach was the first to return to the empty house that day. His regimental lunch at the club had been cut short by a riot outside a nearby factory.

This had put George in a rather bad mood as he returned home, so much so he was still grumbling when he walked into the house.

"That bloody Guardian, stirring up all of this nonsense," he huffed as he came through the door, "Sarah?"

There was no reply. It was dark, and the only light that he could see was the glow of the fire coming from the dining room.

George frowned and lit one of the table lamps. It was much easier to light the table lamps than the wall lamps. He was also aware that Sarah might have fallen asleep. If she had, the light from a table lamp would be much less likely to disturb her.

Once the lamp was lit, he walked from room to room, looking for any signs of Sarah. By the time he had searched the rooms immediately off the entrance hall, Grace had returned from Stickleback Hollow with the footman.

The footman went around the house and lit the lamps in each room. Grace looked confused as she saw the general walking around the hall carrying the lamp.

"Sir, is there something wrong?" Grace asked in a timid voice.

"I can't seem to find Sarah," the brigadier frowned, "can you check her rooms whilst I look for her at the stables?" George asked. Grace nodded and rushed up the stairs to check Sarah's rooms.

The brigadier marched quickly down the hallway and out of the back door to reach the stables. It didn't take him long to discover that not only Sarah wasn't there, but that Black Guy was also missing.

George rushed back to the house. Grace had found nothing in Sarah's room. There was no note, and everything was in its proper place.

The servants began to filter back to the house as the dark afternoon became evening. No one had seen Sarah down in Stickleback Hollow.

The brigadier sent one of the footmen down to the village to fetch Constable Evans whilst he sent another with a telegram to send.

It read:

Alex,

Come back at once. Sarah is missing.

George.

There was no doubt in his mind that Sarah hadn't simply gone out riding. Something was wrong. The entire house was in an uproar by the time Constable Evans arrived.

"Brigadier, we all know that her ladyship is a strong-willed and independent creature. Are you sure she hasn't gone to the lodge and then for a moonlight ride around the estate?" Arwyn asked as he stood in the morning room with the brigadier and Grace.

The brigadier was stood by the fireplace with his face filled with thunder. Grace was sat on one of the sofas softly sobbing.

"What kind of fool do you take me for? If that's what she had done, Sarah would have left a note for Mrs Bosworth or Grace so that a full-scale search wasn't conducted for her. After everything that has happened since she moved here, she has more sense than to simply go off on her own," George roared.

"Very well, who was the last person to see her?" Constable Evans asked.

"I was. It was just before she sent me down to the village with the footman to talk to you," Grace said between sobs.

"Why did she send you to the village to talk to Arwyn?" George asked gruffly.

"Her ladyship wanted me to convince Constable Evans to help us find out what happened to Miss Turner. Our own enquiries weren't getting the answers she hoped for," Grace cried.

"That can't be mere coincidence!" the brigadier shouted, "The only time that she is on her own in the house, and she vanishes."

"Have you seen anyone watching the house?"

Constable Evans asked.

"No, there's been nothing unusual," the brigadier sighed. There was a knock on the morning room door, "Come in," George said with slight resignation.

Mrs Bosworth opened the door to the room.

"I'm sorry to disturb you, brigadier, but one of the parlour maids is missing," Mrs Bosworth said in a worried voice.

"What do you mean missing?" Constable Evans frowned.

"All the staff has come back to the house, it's after six o'clock and Rosie hasn't come back. She's never late. Nobody's seen her and her things are missing from her room," Mrs Bosworth explained.

"No one needed to watch the house; they bribed one of the maids," Arwyn sighed,

"Who did?" Grace squeaked.

"Whoever has taken Lady Sarah. I'll try and find Rosie. See if I can find anything out from her. In the meantime, I suggest we arrange a search party. Have men from the village and as many that can be spared from Grangeback and Duffleton Hall. We send them out over the land and into the

city to see what we can find. If you can reach Mr Hunter -"
Arwyn said.

"I've already sent for him," George assured the
policeman.

"Very good, then I will set out to find Rosie and
organise the men in the village. Can I leave the men of
Grangeback and Duffleton Hall to you, brigadier?" the
constable asked.

"I'll have Bosworth organise the men here and go to
Duffleton directly. Shall we have the men assemble at the
church in two hours?" the brigadier asked.

"Two hours at the church. I will go ask Reverend
Butterfield if he will open the church and arrange some tea for
the men," the constable said. He nodded his head in Grace's
direction and left the morning room.

"Grace, did he agree to help you find Miss Turner?"
the brigadier asked when Arwyn was far enough out of
earshot.

"No, sir. He said that nothing would induce him to
help her ladyship and I short of Almighty God coming down
from heaven and telling him to," Grace sniffed.

"I see. Well, you should go splash your face with cold

water. Then make yourself useful and see what the maids can tell you about Rosie," the brigadier said, dismissing Grace from the room.

Mrs Bosworth stood in the doorway still. She waited until Grace had left before she spoke.

"Brigadier, are you all right?" she asked gently.

"When Sarah and Alex are both back at Grangeback, I will be fine. Until then, Mrs Bosworth, it is not a question I am willing to contemplate," George sighed.

Chapter 12

Two hours passed surprisingly quickly. The Reverend Butterfield opened the church and made sure that there was plenty of tea for the men and even managed to convince the parish secretary, Mrs Franks, to make some hot stew for them.

Men filed in from the village as word spread that Lady Sarah was missing. Stanley and Lee Baker were both there, as was Henry Cartwright, Doctor Hales, Richard Hales and Gordon Hales.

At half-past five, the footmen, grooms, gardeners and Bosworth all came down from Grangeback to the church.

At five minutes to six, the brigadier arrived with Mr Daniel Cooper and the men from Duffleton Hall.

Constable Evans counted the men and made plans to split the group into smaller ones to search. There were enough men for groups of four and five to be sent out. Once Constable Evans had divided the men, the brigadier gave them their assignments.

The brigadier, Doctor Hales, Constable Evans and Lord Cooper were the only men left when the groups have been decided and sent out. The Reverend Butterfield had left the key to the church with Doctor Hales and taken the verger along with Stanley and Lee Baker to search for any signs of Sarah in the farmland that lay on the far side of the village.

"Jack and I will go to Chester and see the Chief Constable tonight. I will petition for him to send his officers out in search of Sarah and to reach out to other police forces around the country," the brigadier said as he watched Mrs Franks taking the empty cups out of the church.

"I will take Constable Evans to see some of my friends in Chester. There are a few gentlemen that may have seen her if she were taken to the city," Daniel said.

"Good, send word to my house if you learn anything," Doctor Hales grunted as Constable Evans and Mr Cooper left the church and set off for Chester in Daniel's carriage.

Daniel didn't tell Arwyn where they were going, and the two didn't say anything as the carriage trundled towards the city. It came to a stop a little before 9pm, and Daniel led Arwyn up the steps of a grand looking premises.

The young lord knocked on the door, and it was opened a few minutes later by a rather distinguished-looking butler.

"Lord Daniel Cooper to see Lord St. Vincent," Daniel said, presenting a card to the butler.

"I'm afraid that Lord St. Vincent is not at home, my lord, but Mr Callum St. Vincent is here. Should I ask him if he is available?" the butler said after he examined the card.

"Please," Daniel said and stepped into the hallway to wait, Arwyn close behind him.

"Do you think that the St. Vincents will have seen her ladyship?" Arwyn asked in a quiet voice.

"They know a great many people in Chester; if anyone has seen her, the St. Vincents will be able to find them," Daniel replied in hushed tones.

It didn't take the butler long to return and escort Arwyn and Lord Cooper to a small drawing room towards the back of the house.

The French windows on the room were open letting in the cold night air. Mr Callum St. Vincent was sat in a high-backed armchair staring out of the open doors to the garden.

"Good evening, Callum," Lord Cooper said as Mr St.

Vincent got out of his chair to greet his visitors.

"Daniel! What a pleasant surprise, I didn't know you were in the city," Callum said as he held out his hand to Daniel.

"I wasn't, something has happened. Do you remember Lady Sarah from Grangeback?" Daniel said as he shook Callum's hand.

"Yes, what's happened?" Callum frowned.

"Her ladyship is missing. She vanished from Grangeback earlier today. We've come into the city to try and find out if you know anyone that may have seen her," Daniel explained.

"Well, that is a serious business. Come, we'll go to the Assembly Rooms, if anyone has seen Lady Sarah they will most likely be there," Callum said with a grin.

The three men made their way to the Assembly Rooms in Daniel's carriage. There were a lot of men engaged in a card tournament in the room, but none of them had seen Sarah, except for Lord St. Vincent.

"I was certain that it was Lady Sarah, she was being escorted to the stage at about 6 o'clock by two men in long coats. I'd never seen them before, but the lady didn't seem to be under duress, so I thought nothing of it," Lord St. Vincent said as he rubbed his chin and furrowed his brow.

"Do you know where the stage was going, my lord?" Arwyn asked.

"London, I believe," Joshua replied.

"Then we shall head to London and see if we can find her," Daniel said firmly.

"If you don't mind, I'll accompany you," Callum said.

"We'll depart at once; I'll send a telegram to the brigadier and Doctor Hales telling them we have gone to London in search of her," Lord Cooper had become surprisingly animated.

Constable Evans remained silent and carefully studied the St. Vincent brothers. There was nothing in their countenance to suggest that either man was lying or wished Sarah any ill, but the policeman still had an uneasy feeling about them both.

Daniel was quick to trust the two men, almost too quick. But there was a chance that Sarah was now in London and the constable was duty-bound to do all that he could to make sure she returned home safely.

Chapter 13

Sarah was carried into the asylum. She tried all that she could to break free from the two men that held her, but even with her clawing and struggling, the two men held fast.

She was taken to a small room that had nothing more than a straw mattress on the floor. Mrs Bird followed the two men carrying a white jacket with sewn-up sleeves that had long ties on the ends of them.

Sarah was forced into the jacket and had the buckles fastened and the straps tied around her back. When it was done up, try as she might, Sarah couldn't break free.

"You are simply wasting your energy. There is no way out of that jacket," Mrs Bird said flatly as she looked at Sarah with a raised eyebrow.

"You can't keep me here," Sarah growled.

"Your brother has had you committed for your own safety. You will remain here until you are no longer a danger," Mrs Bird said firmly.

116

"He is not my brother," Sarah shouted.

"If you continue to behave like this, then we will have to take measures. Your brother is paying for access to better care and facilities whilst you are here. If you don't behave, then you will be treated like everyone else here," Mrs Bird warned.

Sarah scowled at Mrs Bird as the older woman walked out of the room. The door was pulled closed, and Sarah could hear the key turning in the lock.

There was no window in the room she was held in. The floor was cold, and the wall was damp. It was possibly the most wretched place that the lady had ever found herself.

There were poor areas of India she had visited and seen rooms where eight people or more were living in a single room, but in her mind, this place was far worse than that.

She was cold, and there wasn't a blanket in the room. Her cloak had been taken from her shoulders when the straitjacket had been put on. It was lying in a crumpled heap on the floor, but with her hands tied, she couldn't pull it about her to keep out the cold.

She shuffled over on her knees and used her teeth to drag the cloak onto her body as she lay down on the sack of straw.

She felt like crying, but she knew that crying would not help her leave the place she now found herself in. She lay awake for hours trying to think of a way out of the asylum, but knowing almost nothing about the place, there was very little that she could do.

Sarah was woken the next morning by the door to the cell being pulled open. She was escorted out of the room to what looked like a library where a genial looking man sat, waiting for her.

"Good morning, Lady St. Vincent. My name is Doctor Jones. Your brother has been very concerned about your behaviour. You've been brought here so that we can see what we can do about your dangerous habits before we let you go back home," the doctor said with a condescending smile on his face.

Sarah wished she had her purse with her so that she could show the doctor exactly what she thought of his behaviour.

She silently stared at the doctor as the two men pushed her down into one of the large chairs opposite him.

"Now, what is it that has caused you to feel so angry?"

118

the doctor asked.

Sarah didn't reply. She just sat and glared at the doctor.

"I see. Not in a talkative mood. Well, we have different ways of addressing your issues," the doctor said as he picked up a cloth and a bottle of a clear liquid.

He poured the liquid onto the cloth as the two men gripped Sarah by the shoulders, holding her firmly as the doctor walked over. He placed the cloth over her nose and mouth, allowing her to breathe in the fumes.

Sarah felt her mind going cloudy. The next thing that she could remember, she was sat in a room with a woman she recognised.

"Well, well, well, Lady Sarah. What an unpleasant surprise," Miss Turner said. She didn't look like the woman that Sarah remembered from All Hallows' Eve.

Her hair was matted and unwashed. Her skin was waxy and pale. She had lost a lot of weight so that her clothes were just hanging off her.

"Miss Turner!" Sarah said as she tried to sit up but found it virtually impossible whilst her arms were bound.

"He's delivered you here to me, hasn't he? He's given

me a chance to redeem myself by dealing with you within these walls," Miss Turner had an odd expression on her face, it was somewhere between delirium and insanity.

The crazed woman slowly advanced on Sarah, but there was nowhere for the young lady to go. The wall was directly behind her, and she couldn't get to her feet to try to run.

Miss Turner launched at Sarah and wrapped her hands around her the young lady's throat. Sarah's head was already feeling foggy from whatever the doctor had forced her to inhale. The pressure on her throat was causing her vision to darken and pain emanated from her throat where Miss Turner's nails had punctured her skin.

Sarah was only dimly aware of the sound of the door to the room opening and the pain in her throat lessening.

She could tell there was someone else in the room, but whether they were there to help or hurt her, she didn't know. The only thing she wanted to do now was to sleep and wake up to find that being trapped in the asylum was simply a nightmare.

Chapter 14

The brigadier and Doctor Hales went straight to the police house when they arrived in Chester. The Chief Constable wasn't there as he was at court, but the police constable assured them that he would be returning soon.

The two men waited in the backroom by the fireplace. Doctor Hales sat in a chair and read the evening edition of the paper. George paced in front of the fire with his hands cupped behind his back.

Every few seconds, he glanced up at the clock that sat on the mantelpiece and shook his head before he resumed pacing again.

When the Chief Constable finally arrived, they had only been waiting for twenty minutes, but to see the look on the brigadier's face, it had seemed more like hours to him.

"Gentlemen, what can I do for you? Constable McIntyre said that you were waiting but didn't say why," Captain Jonnes Smith greeted the two men with a handshake each and a warm smile.

"We are in need of your help, captain; Lady Montgomery Baird Watson-Wentworth is missing. She disappeared from Grangeback this afternoon and hasn't been seen since. One of the parlour maids is also missing." George said worriedly.

"I see, and you are sure that her ladyship isn't out riding or has taken a trip to London?" the Chief Constable frowned.

"No, it appears not. The estate and village have been thoroughly searched. Men from Duffleton Hall, Grangeback and Stickleback Hollow are all out searching for her; but we have come to request your aid in searching the city for her," the doctor explained calmly from the chair.

"I see, well then I will ask Constable McIntyre and Constable Cantello to conduct some enquiries. I assume that Constable Evans is already helping you," Captain Jonnes Smith replied.

"He and Lord Cooper are calling upon some gentlemen in the city to see if they have seen her ladyship," Doctor Hales said, folding the paper and standing up.

"Very good, if you discover anything new, then please

let me know. I wish I could do more to assist you, but with a limited number of constables and the city streets to patrol, these two are all that I can spare right now," the Chief Constable said apologetically.

George opened his mouth to say something, but Doctor Hales steered him out of the police house before the brigadier could say something that he was going to regret.

"There's no point," the doctor hissed in George's ear, "we have some help, and Mr Hunter will have received your message by now. We should return to my house and see what news there is from Constable Evans."

The brigadier begrudgingly agreed and followed the doctor back to his carriage. The two trundled through the night, back to Stickleback Hollow. George leaned back in his seat and closed his eyes, wondering how long it would be until Alex returned.

Mr Hunter was sat in front of a fire, gazing into the flames that danced in the grate. He was staying at the lodge with one of the groundskeepers on the Dall Estate in the highlands Perthshire.

He hadn't gone back to the estate where Heather was. He didn't want to see her. He hadn't been all that interested in her in the first place. She had thrown herself at the hunter, and though it was flattering, she was rather dull compared to Sarah.

Alex sighed and shook his head as he tried to shake himself out of sour mood he had descended into since leaving England.

He kept replaying the fight with Sarah over in his mind, which only served to worsen his mood. Andrew Brendan was the groundskeeper on the Dall Estate, and he had left Alex to his brooding.

The hunter had barely uttered two words to the groundskeeper since he had arrived and each evening was an uncomfortable exercise in enduring unbroken silences.

Brendan had taken to walking around the estate late at night when the silence between the two men became too much. Pattinson spent his days lying at Alex's feet, but when Brendan went out to walk during the evenings, the dog would pad alongside him.

As he returned to the lodge that night, Pattinson began to growl. Brendan turned to see a messenger racing across the lawn clutching a telegram in his hand.

"What is it, lad?" Brendan asked in a gruff voice.

"There's a telegram for Mr Hunter," the boy said breathlessly.

"How did they find him here?" Brendan asked.

"Mr Franks rode over with it. It went to him first," the boy said.

"I see, well give it here, I'll make sure Mr Hunter gets it," Brendan said, holding out his hand to the boy.

"Yes, Mr Brendan," the boy squeaked and thrust the paper into the groundskeepers open hand, then ran off back towards the main house.

Brendan went through the door of the lodge and found Alex sat in front of the fire, where he'd left him.

"Hunter, telegram for you," Brendan said as he clattered through the door and kicked off his boots. Alex frowned and got out of the chair he was sat in to take the telegram from Brendan.

Come at once if convenient. If inconvenient, come all the same. Sarah is missing.

"I have to go," Alex said as he read the words on the page. He felt his heart drop as his eyes scanned over the words, and the urgency of them sank in.

He didn't wait for Brendan to say anything. Instead, he gathered his saddlebags from the room he was sleeping in and went out to saddle Harald. Pattinson following gladly at his side.

Chapter 15

When Alex arrived at Grangeback, only Cooky and Mrs Bosworth were there to greet him.

"Mr Hunter, where on earth have you been?" Cooky scolded him.

"It doesn't matter," Alex replied. He had his saddlebags flung over his shoulder as he walked through the kitchen door.

"The brigadier is at Doctor Hales' house. The men from Duffleton Hall, Stickleback Hollow and Grangeback, are all out looking for Sarah. They won't be back until much later," Mrs Bosworth explained.

"Grace is upstairs, but the other maids have all gone home," Cooky told Mr Hunter as she tried to take the saddlebags from him.

"I'll go talk to Grace; then I will go see the brigadier," Alex said bluntly.

He let Cooky take the saddlebags as he made his way

through the house and up the stairs to Grace's room. Pattinson stayed behind in the kitchen and annoyed Cooky until she relented and fed him the leftover table scraps.

He knocked lightly on the door but didn't wait for her to give him permission to enter. The blonde girl was lying on her bed, staring at the ceiling. Alex had imagined that he would find the girl crying into her pillow, but she seemed perfectly calm to him.

"Mr Hunter, you came back," she said in a hollow voice. She didn't turn her head to look at him, just carried on staring at the roof above.

"I want you to tell me everything you know," Alex said as he leaned against a wall on the opposite side of the room.

Grace sighed and then began to tell Alex everything that had happened since he had left for Scotland.

When she had finished, Mr Hunter left without a word. He went down to the stables and took one of the carriage horses to ride. Harald had travelled enough for one day and deserved to rest whilst Alex went to work.

He decided it would be better to leave Pattinson behind for the moment. It had been a long trek from Scotland, and the dog had trotted alongside the horse the whole way.

Alex would need to check over the dog very carefully to make sure he wasn't any the worse for the long journey.

It was a little before midnight by the time Mr Hunter reached Doctor Hales' house.

The brigadier opened the door and was relieved to see his son standing on the doorstep. George told Alex everything that had happened with their meeting with the chief constable and the message from Daniel and Arwyn that told them they were following Sarah's trail to London.

Mr Hunter had yet to step inside the house. He stood and patiently listened to everything the brigadier had to say before he made any form of response.

"I will be in London before lunchtime."

It was all that needed to be said. George nodded and watched Alex turn from Doctor Hales' door.

The sound of horses coming down the road stopped Alex after he'd only taken three steps from the door.

"Hunter? Is that you?" a familiar voice called out as the sound of hoofs on the road ceased.

"Thomas?" Alex called out.

"Well, we should have known that you would be here as well," Edward's voice drifted out of the night.

"What are you both doing out at this hour?" Alex asked.

"The gossips of Chester are talking of Lady Sarah's disappearance and nothing else. With so many engaged in the search, our beloved cousin sent us in search of you," Thomas explained.

"Your cousin?" Alex frowned as he moved through the darkness to where the two men had stopped.

"Lady Szonja. She wants to talk to you," Edward grinned at his school friend.

"Why would she want to talk to me?" Alex looked even more confused than before.

"She spoke to Lady Sarah before she disappeared. She came to visit her whilst we were shooting," Edward explained.

"Why would that have anything to do with her wanting to see me?" Alex asked.

"Well, we can't say for certain, but there is a rumour circulating," Thomas said slyly.

"You're both being rather frustrating; can you tell me what is going on in plain English? It's been a long day, and I need to get to London." Alex couldn't hide the edge in his voice.

"Lady Sarah was seen in Chester the day she disappeared," Thomas replied.

"I know, the brigadier told me," Alex said with mounting annoyance.

"Did he tell you that Lord St. Vincent told him he saw Sarah being taken by two men?" Edward asked.

"He did," Alex said; his patience almost exhausted.

"The rumour says something different. The rumour says that Lady Sarah was seen in the company of Lord St. Vincent and no one else," Thomas continued.

"So Lady Szonja wants to see you," Edward finished.

"Lead the way," Alex replied.

Chapter 16

Edward and Thomas led the way across the fields

that lay between the lands of Tatton Park and Stickleback
Hollow. It wasn't a short journey, but it was much quicker to
ride over the fields than it was to stick to the roads.

Alex was glad he'd left Harald and Pattinson back at
Grangeback, the added distance from Stickleback Hollow to
Tatton Park might have been more than either of the two
animals could take.

It was a little after 1 o'clock in the morning when the
three men arrived at the great house at Tatton Park. The house
was dark, except for the lamps that burned outside the front of
the main door, a light that was coming from the drawing
room.

Edward took the horses from Thomas and Alex, then
led them away to the stable whilst Thomas took Alex into the
house.

Thomas walked briskly but quietly, all of the

household were in bed, so the house seemed to be deserted.

He led Alex to the drawing room and knocked softly on the door before opening it. The countess was sat in the room wearing an ornate dressing gown over her nightdress. Her hair was plaited to the side of her face and lay over her shoulder.

"Mr Hunter, thank you for coming. Please sit down." the countess said. For the late hour, the Lady Szonja didn't look tired. Her face was an emotionless mask as she spoke, and her voice didn't betray the slightest emotion.

Thomas pointed Alex towards one of the long sofas, and the two men sat down beside each other. Edward appeared a few minutes later and sat down in one of the chairs.

When all three men were seated, the countess began to speak.

"How much do you know about Lord St. Vincent?" she asked. Her hands were folded in her lap, and she was sat perfectly still.

"I know that he has some connection to Lady de Mandeville and has business interests in the Far East. I know that he was engaged to Miss Turner and I suspect that he's been in Chester since All Hallows' Eve," said Mr Hunter slowly.

"I see, that's more than I expected. His connection to Lady de Mandeville is one that you should be especially wary of. It is something that grants him a lot of protection. He knows that if he finds himself in trouble, the duchess will be there to assist him," Lady Szonja explained.

"What does that have to do with Lady Sarah Montgomery Baird Watson-Wentworth's disappearance?" Alex asked.

"It sadly has more to do with it than I would like. I didn't tell Sarah when I met her, but I was a great friend to her parents. Her mother was a rather striking beauty in her youth, and I always greatly admired her," Lady Szonja began.

"You knew her parents?" Alex frowned.

"I did, her mother was a distant cousin of my late husband. She came to my wedding and I, in turn, attended hers. We used to write to each other about a great many things. When Colonel Montgomery Baird was posted to India, it broke my heart to see them go," the countess shook her head sadly.

"Did you ever visit them in India?" Edward asked.

"No, the count was not a man suited to hot climates, and he didn't approve of me travelling to India alone. Even to see my dear friend when Sarah was born. She still wrote to me, but her letters changed after a time. The tone of them was different and stilted, and even her choice of words was strange," Szonja recounted.

"How quickly did things change?" Alex asked.

"It was around three months after she went to India. I grew greatly concerned as there were multiple references to dates, figures, facts, most of which I had never come across before. She mentioned events that had never happened and gave dates and names that meant nothing to me. I received three letters that were all very similar before I wrote a reply. I expressed great concern for her and asked if there was anything I might be able to do for her. She replied that she had all she needed in her King James Bible that I had presented her with at her Christening," Lady Szonja replied.

"But how could you have been at her Christening?" Thomas frowned.

"That was the very question I asked myself. I asked my husband about the bible in question, and he told me that it had been the same bible that he had been given at his Christening.

It was a family tradition. Then my husband said something very odd. He told me that it was funny, I was asking about it as it was very common for the bible being used to create a book cypher to send secret messages. It was a trick that his uncle had taught all the children in his family, including Cynthia," Lady Szonja said.

"A book cypher?" Alex frowned.

"All the dates and facts and figures that were mentioned were all part of the code. I used my husband's bible to decrypt the page, line and word to reveal what was hidden in those letters and then replied in kind," the countess smiled.

"What was in the letters?" Alex asked quickly.

"You can see for yourself," Lady Szonja said as she picked up a leather satchel from down the side of the sofa and handed it to the hunter.

"Are these all her letters?" Alex asked as he opened the satchel and started to leaf through all the papers that were contained within.

"They are. I gave Sarah the same bible when she was christened. It should be in her rooms at Grangeback. You will be able to decode the letters for yourself. But in brief, they detailed how Cynthia and Stephen had met Lady de Mandeville, what she was like, the influence she had and the activities they were being drawn into. To begin with, it wasn't criminal activity per se, but there were some very questionable practices that were being employed, and Cynthia never felt safe around her. She felt like she was constantly being watched," Lady Szonja said.

"Lady de Mandeville has a great many connections in India and here in Britain. It wouldn't be all that difficult for her to monitor letters that were leaving India, even twenty years ago," Edward added.

"Then the business with the opium and China began," Lady Szonja's eyes twinkled.

"Opium?" Alex tilted his head and looked at the countess intently.

"You are aware of the difficulties with opium in China?" the countess asked.

"I know that the import of opium into China is illegal and that traders on the Chinese coast are buying the opium from independent merchants that are not as independent as they may appear," Alex replied slowly.

"You are very well informed, Mr Hunter. A man-made

for political life perhaps, but I digress. Yes, most of the independent merchants that sell the East India Company grown opium to the Chinese traders are employed by Lady de Mandeville. A great many people have grown rich off the trade, and more flock to her to make their fortune. This is how she has amassed her great fortune that allows her to influence the politics of not only India and China but also Britain herself," Lady Szonja explained.

"How can a woman influence the politics of three nations by simply amassing a fortune?" Thomas asked.

"She is not only rich; she is bored, clever and exceptionally dangerous. You will see in those letters. But the material point of it all is that Lord St. Vincent was a man of nothing more than a title creaking under debt before he began working for Lady de Mandeville. Now he is rich, powerful and one of her greatest assets; especially when it comes to finding young, ambitious men that want to forge a name for themselves and step out from under the shadow of their fathers and brothers. He is also very good at finding young women that have even rarer qualities." the countess said as she leaned back on the sofa.

"Which Lady de Mandeville would value even more,"

Alex said, shaking his head.

"Precisely," Lady Szonja agreed.

"Why would women be more valuable to Lady de Mandeville?" Edward frowned.

"Because there are many who underestimate women, dismiss them as hysterical and little more than wallflowers. Women that can take advantage of this make excellent spies, manipulators, blackmailers and even assassins," Alex explained.

"And are easily disposed of once their usefulness has expired," Lady Szonja finished.

"I see, so how does this help with the disappearance of Lady Sarah?" Thomas asked.

"Lord St. Vincent was seen in her company before she disappeared. I am told that Mr Callum St. Vincent has accompanied Lord Daniel Cooper and Constable Evans to London, helping them to search for Sarah. The brothers are behind her disappearance, of that I have no doubt, and she has been removed on the orders of Lady de Mandeville," the countess said firmly.

"But Sarah knows nothing; she's not interested in political intrigue or the business of the Far East," Alex shook his head in frustration.

"That is clearly not how Lady de Mandeville sees things. Tread carefully, Mr Hunter, I believe that she may also try to remove you from this picture as well. Read the letters, but trust very few with the information within. Thomas, Edward, make sure that Mr Hunter gets home safely," Lady Szonja said.

On the ride back, Alex felt sick to his stomach. He was tired and half-hoped that Sarah's disappearance would still turn out to be a simple misunderstanding. He didn't go back to the lodge, but instead made his way to Grangeback.

The household was filled with men that had been searching for Sarah and found nothing. Discussions were detailing where they would look next and what time would be best to begin searching again.

Pattinson lolloped over to his master as Mr Hunter stepped through the door. Alex didn't say a word to anyone as he strode through the house to the back stairs and made his way to Sarah's room.

He searched through her books until he found the bible with an inscription that related to her Christening. It didn't bear Lady Szonja's name, but it was the only bible that he could find.

Pattinson lay down next to Mr Hunter as he began to decipher the letters, occasionally flicking his eyes over to the door and lifting his head when someone passed by the doors.

Alex was only disturbed once. Mrs Bosworth came at the break of dawn to open the curtains and found Mr Hunter with his head buried in papers.

She didn't understand what he was doing, but she knew what the look of determination on his face meant.

"I'll leave food outside the door for you," was all she said.

Chapter 17

With the men off searching for Sarah, there wasn't much for Cooky to do at Grangeback. She made several things to keep in the larder – pork pies, steak and kidney pudding, apple pie, a few cooked chickens – all of them could be served by the maids and eaten cold when the men came back to the house.

But there were no grand dinners to be cooked and very little that she could do after she had prepared the mountain of cold foods.

Cooky was not a woman that enjoyed being useless, which is exactly how she had felt since Sarah had disappeared.

There was no one to comfort and nothing she could do to bring Sarah back from wherever she had gone. So Cooky decided that rather than sit around the house and worry, she would go to Chester.

She loved visiting the markets, whether flowers or food, there was nothing that made her happier than when she was at a market. With so little to be done at Grangeback, it was the perfect opportunity to spend most of the day exploring the different stalls and haggling with the vendors.

Cooky had even started to take an interest in spices from India. She listened to Lady Sarah talk about the different foods that she had grown up eating and how strange the English meals were compared to what she was used to.

Cooky had decided that she would find the ingredients to make a curry for Lady Sarah for her first night back at Grangeback.

She was stood examining the different types of rice that were on offer on one particular stall when something strange caught her eye.

Rosie was stood in the middle of the market building, looking anxiously about. Cooky couldn't quite believe that the girl was stood there. She seemed to be very agitated, but she hadn't spotted the cook from Grangeback.

Cooky moved to stand behind one of the pillars that would keep her out of sight; she pulled a small mirror out of her pocket so that she could keep an eye on what Rosie was doing.

It wasn't a mirror of any real value or aesthetic beauty, but the cook liked to keep it close so that she could check her face and hair for any flecks of food or liquids after she had been cooking.

A few minutes passed, and a well-dressed gentleman appeared with a young woman beside him.

"Come, we need to talk somewhere a little quieter," the man replied in an authoritative voice.

"No, sir, I'd rather stay here and talk," Rosie said nervously.

"This is the creature that you've been relying on?" the second woman said in disgust. There was a slight lit to her voice that Cooky couldn't place.

"She managed to see that Lady Sarah came to meet me without anyone finding out. She did her job well. You, Heather, failed to keep Mr Hunter in Scotland on two occasions." the gentleman said coldly.

"I did all I could to make that man fall in love with me. It's worked on all the others you've sent to me." Heather snorted defensively.

"Though clearly not this time." the man replied curtly.

"All I needed was another week," Heather replied, waving her hand.

"He didn't even go back to you when he left

Grangeback. I did all I could to use Daniel as a wedge to drive them apart, and he didn't even turn to you for comfort. We need to find that watch. Hunter knows where it is. Rosie, you're to take Heather to the house to see Hunter. Heather, you are going to get him to leave with you and tell you where the pocket watch is." the young gentleman hissed.

"And what is it that you'll be doing?" Heather demanded.

"I will be making sure that no one finds out that we have the girl locked up in the asylum," the man replied hotly.

"I can't go back to the house. They'll have me arrested, and they'll ask me questions. I can't go to prison," Rosie whined as she grabbed hold of the man's arm.

"Shhh, it's all going to be fine. You don't need to go into the house. Just take Heather there. Make sure that she doesn't get lost. Then you can come back to me, and I will take you away from all of this. We'll go to India, and you'll be safe," the man soothed as he stroked Rosie's hair.

The young maid gulped down her tears.

"Well then, let's be off. I don't have all day to waste," Heather snapped at Rosie.

Cooky didn't move from her place behind the pillar

until she was sure that Rosie was out of sight. She didn't know how long it was going to take Rosie and Heather to get to Grangeback, but she was certain that the curry for Lady Sarah was going to have to wait.

Cooky told the carriage driver she would make him double dinner rations for a week if he could get her back to Grangeback before the hour was out.

It took much less than an hour for the small carriage to reach the great house, and Cooky wasted no time in finding Alex.

She rushed up to Sarah's room and flung open the doors to find Lady Szonja sat on one of the sofas with a copy of the bible in her hand, and Alex on the floor amongst a great pile of papers.

"Cooky? What is it?" Alex asked with a frown as he looked over at the flustered cook.

"I'm sorry, Mr Hunter, I didn't know you had company. It's just that there's news for you, about Lady Sarah," Cooky gasped for breath. At the mention of Sarah's name, Alex leapt to his feet and rushed over to the cook.

"What news?" Alex asked as he gently placed his hands on Cooky's shoulders.

146

"Rosie, the maid that went missing. She was in the market in Chester. She met with a tall, well-dressed man. I don't know who he was, but there was a girl called Heather with him," Cooky began.

"Heather?" Alex dropped his arms and stepped back from Cooky, looking confused.

"Yes, they were talking about a pocket watch and keeping you in Scotland away from Lady Sarah. The man said something about using Mr Cooper to drive a wedge between you," Cooky said as Alex put his head in his hands.

"Where are they now?" he asked as he pulled himself together.

"Rosie is bringing Heather here. The man told her to take you back to Scotland and to find out where the pocket watch is," Cooky said hurriedly.

"If they are coming here, then -" Alex began.

"Then I will be there to greet them. Leave the ladies to me," the countess smiled as she gracefully rose from the sofa and glided to the door.

"I need to find out who that man was and where Sarah is," Alex said to himself as he made to step past Cooky.

"She's in the asylum," Cooky unintentionally shouted

the information.

"What?" Alex looked at the cook with disbelief.

"The man said she was there. He didn't say her name, but I am sure he meant Lady Sarah," Cooky assured Mr Hunter.

"If she is there, then Arwyn is wasting his time in London. Can one of the boys carry a message to London? An express will take too long to find Arwyn, and I have no idea where to send a telegram," Alex asked.

"I'll have one of Doctor Hales' boys take it. They know London well; they'll be able to find Constable Evans without any problem." Cooky said firmly.

"Good. Tell whichever one of them that they are to give this to Constable Evans and no one else," Alex said as he took a blank piece of paper and began scribbling on it.

Once he was done writing, he pressed the paper into Cooky's hand.

"Where are you going?" Cooky asked.

"To Chester, to tell the Chief Constable where Sarah is," Alex replied over his shoulder.

Cooky watched the young man rush away with a frown on her face. She looked down at the piece of paper in her hand. It read,

Arwyn,

Come back at once. Sarah is not in London. She is being held in an asylum, I assume it is the Cheshire Asylum, but that will be for the police to investigate. Cooky overheard Rosie meeting with a man that I think was Lord St. Vincent and a woman that had been sent to take me back to Scotland. John Smith is hard at work, it seems. I will tell you more when you are back.

Hunter

P.S. Don't show this note to Daniel and Callum.

The cook frowned as she read the letter. It didn't make much sense to her, but she hoped that it would make some sense to Constable Evans. She carefully folded the paper and sent one of the footmen to fetch either Richard or Gordon Hales from Stickleback Hollow. She didn't particularly care which boy came to take the letter, only that one of them

The Mysteries of Stickleback Hollow: Mr Daniel Cooper of Stickleback Hollow

would.

Chapter 18

Captain Jonnes Smith was not a man that enjoyed having his day interrupted by the continuing misadventures of a single young lady.

When Alex arrived at the police house in Chester, the Chief Constable had tried to turn him away and send him off to meet Brigadier Webb-Kneelingroach and Doctor Hales at the doctor's home.

However, Mr Hunter was far more stubborn and persistent than the Chief Constable gave him credit for. After making Alex wait for three hours, the Chief Constable finally agreed to meet with him.

"Mr Hunter, we really are doing everything we can. I know you are a close friend of the family -" Captain Jonnes Smith began as Alex was shown into the room where he was sat.

"Chief Constable, you don't quite understand why I am here. I am not here to ask you what has been done or what you have found," Alex said gruffly.

"Oh? Then why are you here, Mr Hunter?" Captain Jonnes Smith leaned forward with interest as he spoke.

"I am bringing you new evidence," Alex replied.

"Evidence?" the Chief Constable frowned.

"Rosie, the maid from Grangeback, was seen meeting with two individuals in the market today," Alex explained.

"I see, and who was it that saw the maid?" Captain Jonnes Smith asked wearily.

"Cooky. May I continue?" Alex asked matching the Chief Constable's tone.

"I see; very well," he allowed.

"Cooky overheard their conversation. Lady Sarah is being kept locked away in an asylum. It was arranged by the gentleman. Cooky didn't say who, only that he was well-dressed," Alex continued.

"I see; that is very interesting news. Did she happen to overhear which asylum?" the Chief Constable asked.

"No, though I suspect it is the Cheshire County Lunatic Asylum. It's the closest one," Alex replied.

"You may be right, Mr Hunter. Very well, we will investigate this. Though I would appreciate it if -"

Before the Chief Constable could finish his sentiment,

the door to the office was flung open, and George and Jack marched into the room.

"Alex! Cooky showed us your note before Richard rode to London with it. She told us everything she saw," George said hurriedly as he laid eyes on the hunter.

"Gentlemen, please," the Chief Constable said with frustration as he rose from his seat.

"Thomas, this is not the time for delaying. I'm a doctor, I know the physician at the asylum. Gordon has gone to fetch him here for us. We're going there tonight," Doctor Hales instructed in the sternest tone he possessed.

"Jack, there are the courts to consider," Captain Jonnes Smith replied evenly. Not even a man like Doctor Hales could intimidate the Chief Constable.

"Preposterous. Jones is a good man, he'll tell us straight out if we're barking up the wrong tree," Jack said dismissively.

It didn't take long for Gordon to arrive with Doctor Jones in tow. The asylum doctor looked rather perplexed at being summoned, but his demeanour brightened immediately when he saw Doctor Hales.

"Jack! What is all this? Your boy appeared and told me

I had to come here with no other explanation," Doctor Jones frowned as he shook Doctor Hales by the hand.

"It's a delicate matter; we thought it best to talk here, away from prying eyes and ears," Jack said warmly.

"Well, whatever I can do to help will be done. You know that I'm always here to help," Jones said as he looked from Alex to the brigadier to Captain Jonnes Smith.

"My ward has been kidnapped, and we have reason to believe that she is being held at your asylum," George began without any thought of tact.

The demeanour of Doctor Jones changed immediately.

"None of my patients are the victims of kidnapping. What a terrible allegation to make, they are brought to me by their friends and family. They are there to escape the city and the pressures of their lives that have led to mental imbalance. My asylum is not a prison," he scowled at the brigadier and spoke with an acid tongue.

"Well then, there is no possibility that Lady Sarah Montgomery Baird Watson-Wentworth is there?" the Chief Constable asked dryly.

"None whatsoever. I only accept family members bringing in patients," Doctor Jones was adamant as he spoke.

"Thank you, doctor, I am sure Master Hales will see you back home," the Chief Constable said.

Brigadier Webb-Kneelingroach, Doctor Hales, Mr Hunter and Gordon Hales all followed Doctor Jones out of the Chief Constable's office.

"Before you go, doctor, have there been any new arrivals at your asylum in the last few days?" Mr Hunter asked.

"There has been one, yes," Doctor Jones frowned.

"A woman of rank?" Alex asked.

"She is from a well-connected family," the doctor said slowly.

"A relation of Lord St. Vincent?" Mr Hunter continued and the colour drained from the face of Doctor Jones.

"My God, she kept telling me she wasn't his sister. I thought it was just a mental break down," Doctor Jones stammered.

"Then Sarah is at your asylum!" George cried with relief.

"She is, but there was an incident with another patient. It's too much to explain here. Come, I'll take you to the asylum directly," Doctor Jones said and led Gordon and George out of

155

the police station. Doctor Hales made to follow but noticed that Mr Hunter was hanging back.

"Are you not coming?" Jack asked.

"No, I need to collect my things from Sarah's room before she returns to Grangeback," Alex replied.

"Very well," the doctor frowned.

"Whilst you are there, could you ask Doctor Jones for the admission paperwork? It could be very enlightening," Alex asked.

"Of course, I will bring it to the lodge this evening," the doctor agreed, "you should be there to bring her home, you know. Without you, we wouldn't have found her," Jack said gently.

"Without Cooky we wouldn't have found her. Be grateful that she loves markets so much," Alex grinned in reply.

"You honestly don't want to be there?" Jack asked.

"I think it is best that I am not," Alex said firmly.

"I think you're wrong. Sometimes in life women have a choice between men that they are expected to marry and men that are worthy of marrying them," the doctor replied

"And sometimes we have to forget about what we

want for the happiness of those we care about," Alex countered.

"I see that you are as stubborn as your mother was. I will not press the matter further. Until this evening," Doctor Hales said and left Mr Hunter standing in the police house, trying not to think on the incident that Doctor Jones had mentioned.

Chapter 19

Sarah lay in a hospital bed. She was strapped down with thick leather straps that she had long since stopped trying to break.

She didn't know exactly how long she had been there, but it felt like aeons had passed. She had been left largely unhurt by the attack of Annabel Turner, but the doctor had chosen to have her restrained just in case.

She was beginning to feel that she would never be able to set foot outside of the asylum when she heard a familiar voice calling her name.

"Sarah? Sarah? My God, what are you doing to her? Have these straps removed at once." the brigadier barked as he strode over to her bedside.

"George, you're here!" Sarah was so relieved to see her guardian that she started to cry.

"It's all alright, my dear, you are safe now. We'll take you home, and you can tell us what happened," the brigadier soothed as the straps were unfastened. Gordon and George

helped Sarah to stand and held her up as she tentatively walked across the infirmary.

Doctor Jones apologised to Sarah profusely as he returned her belongings and made plans to meet with Doctor Hales for a hand or two of bridge before the month was out.

Leaving the asylum was a rather surreal experience for Sarah; she couldn't quite believe that she was free, or that her guardian had found her.

When they reached Grangeback, Cooky and Mrs Bosworth were both waiting on the steps of the great house along with Grace.

The lady's maid helped her mistress into the house and got her ready for bed. As Sarah was walking up the stairs, she could have sworn that Alex was stood watching her from the library door, but when she looked a second time, there was no one there.

It wasn't until the following day that Sarah related her tale in full to the brigadier and Grace. Doctor Hales had left not long after they had arrived back, and Gordon had gone to spread the news that Sarah had been found.

Throughout the day, the men returned to Stickleback Hollow, Duffleton Hall and Grangeback, including Lord

Daniel Cooper and Constable Evans.

Grace went down into the village to tell Arwyn what had happened in his absence, and Daniel came to call on Sarah.

Callum St. Vincent returned to the rooms his brother had taken in Chester to find Joshua in a foul temper.

"It was Hunter, wasn't it?" Lord St. Vincent growled as his brother entered the room.

"He sent a letter to the constable with one of the young men from the village," Callum confirmed.

"Damn him!" Joshua yelled and threw his half-drunk glass of whisky at the fireplace. The glass shattered against the cast iron hearth, and the liquid caused the flames to flare for a moment before returning to normal.

"What happened to Heather keeping him in Scotland?" Callum frowned.

"She failed. John Smith sent me this," Lord St. Vincent said as he dramatically thrust a telegram in Callum's direction.

Joshua

Rarely has anyone dared to disappointment in such a way, not once, but twice. Business dictates that you are to both return at once to my company. Bring the maid. She will be a pleasant enough distraction for you. I hear that your former fiancée is most unwell and that the heather was lost in a freak landslide. Most unfortunate.

Yours in distaste,

JS

"What will she do to us?" Callum asked nervously as he finished ready the missive.

"At this point, I don't know. For the moment, we are both too valuable to the company, and she is a woman that places business above all other things. But she is also a woman that never forgets. The moment our usefulness expires, so shall we," Joshua sighed.

"Then we must do our best to ensure that never happens," Callum said firmly, "do you know how she found out so quickly?"

"No, but whoever is sending her the information knew

before you arrived back that Sarah had been found," Joshua replied in frustration.

News soon spread to Alex's ears that Lord and Mr St. Vincent were returning to India. He felt a great sense of relief, though he knew that it wouldn't last very long.

Lady Szonja came with the news and also to tell the hunter that she was returning home.

"I will keep my ears open for anything that may be of interest to you," she said before she took her leave of him.

"What happened to Heather and Rosie?" he asked.

"I wouldn't worry too much about either of them anymore," was all the countess had said in reply.

Arwyn came to visit the hunter around lunchtime so that the two men could discuss all that had happened in great detail.

"So the woman that was chasing you in Scotland and caused Sarah to dismiss you, she was working for Lord St. Vincent?" Arwyn asked, shaking his head.

"So it seems. She may not have done what she was instructed to, but she certainly managed to separate me from Sarah," Mr Hunter sighed.

"So, in the future, we must be more careful," Arwyn

162

shrugged.

"There is also this," Alex said as he handed a piece of paper to Arwyn.

"What is it?" Constable Evans frowned.

"The admission papers for Sarah for the asylum," Alex sighed.

"Mrs Sarah Hunter? Signed by Mr Harry Taylor?" Arwyn screwed up his face in confusion.

"Harry always did find himself rather amusing," Alex sighed.

"You think he was involved in this?" Arwyn asked.

"It's possible; after all, I don't know who the gentleman was that Cooky saw. It could have been Harry or Joshua," Alex shrugged.

"Well, the only thing we can do now is watch, and wait. Grace will help keep Sarah safe. She seems to have adjusted well to having an unorthodox mistress," Arwyn grinned.

"Unorthodox is one word for it," Grace said from behind the two men. Alex and Arwyn turned to see Grace and Sarah stood just outside the open back door.

"Constable Evans, would you be kind enough to walk

me to the lake, I am told it should be frozen by now," Grace asked with a slight smile.

"Of course, good day Hunter," Arwyn nodded at Alex and stepped out of the lodge to accompany Grace.

"May I come in?" Sarah asked in a quiet voice.

"Of course," Alex said quickly. Pattinson had been asleep by the fire, but the sound of Sarah's voice stirred him from his slumber.

The great beast yawned and trotted over to sit at the feet of the lady until she knelt down to fuss him.

"I came to apologise for my behaviour, for what I said to you. It was unjust, and it was not what you deserved," Sarah said as she focused her attention on Pattinson.

"There's no need to apologise," Alex insisted.

"There is every need. Since my parents died, I have felt terribly alone. When I first came to England, I didn't know what to expect. I hated London, I was certain that I would never find anywhere to belong here and then there was Grangeback, and Stickleback Hollow, and you," Sarah said standing up and looking Alex in the eyes as she spoke.

"You don't need to say anything," Mr Hunter said adamantly.

"I'm afraid I do. You see, you have been there since I first stumbled into trouble. You have protected me and saved me, but that has to stop," Sarah said firmly.

"Oh?" Alex felt his heart sinking in his chest.

"You can't keep protecting me from these dangers. You need to tell me about them so they can be faced, not hide me away," Sarah insisted.

"I promised George," Alex replied, "Until there is someone else to take care of you, I will always be there."

"I see. Speaking of which, Daniel came to see me yesterday, whilst Grace went to visit Arwyn. He asked me to marry him," Sarah announced.

"I see; I hope you will both be very happy together," Alex replied mechanically.

"I refused him," Sarah smiled.

"What? Why? You know that your position means that you need to be -" Alex half-shouted and Sarah started laughing.

"You are such a fool, Mr Hunter. But a fool I am prepared to wait for," Sarah said gently and left the stunned Mr Hunter stood in the lodge, not knowing quite what to do.

Historical Note

Though many will think of Manners Makyth Man as belonging to Kingsmen, it is actually from the work of William Horman who was the headmaster at Eton and then Winchester in the 15th century. Winchester College still has "manners makyth man" as its motto. The phrase means that politeness and etiquette are what prevent is from falling into savagery.

Electrical Telegraphy was being experimented with by a few different inventors in England, Russia and Germany and by 1852 National telegraphy systems were operated in most countries. In 1838 the telegraph system of Cooke and Whetstone was only a year old and was the first commercial telegraph to be installed in the world. It was installed on the Great Western Railway between Paddington Station and West Drayton. There was no national system at this point in time, but much like the establishment of the Cheshire police force, I have introduced the national telegraph system slightly early to help with telling this story.

In the 19th century there was an increase of private hunting estates that led to a rise in the number of red deer that have caused a myriad of ecological problems in at least the last 150 years, if not longer. I chose to include this in the opening chapter of the book as it is entirely possible that the effects were being to show as early as 1838. Mr Hunter's warnings as to the problems it will cause are just some of the effects that have been seen in Scotland since that time. The red deer over-population continues to this day, and if it remains in such a state, the destructive impact on the ecology will only continue.

The first 40 years of the 1800s were the wettest on record, and 1838 snow fell in London as early as 13th October. For the purpose of this story, I have delayed snowfall in the north until the 1st day of Advent.

The police whistle was used from around 1820; however, it was not something that was given out as standard equipment. It was only used in very special circumstances. It wasn't until the 1880s that the Manchester Metropolitan force and the

Liverpool Police were issued with whistles. The whistle that Sarah presented to Constable Evans would have been a round pea whistle, not the J Hudson & Co whistle that most people associate with the Victorian police.

It is true that all descendants of George II need to seek royal permission to marry. Though this has been relaxed for those who are further down the line of succession in modern times, it would still have been strictly enforced during the Victorian Era, and is rather a cunning way to play for time.

The Cheshire County Lunatic Asylum was opened in September of 1829. The Matron on the hospital was indeed a Mrs Bird, LI. Jones M.D. was the doctor, and Mr W. Rose was the medical superintendent. The asylum housed 50 to 60 people. Men were kept in the south wing and women in the north. For those who belonged to higher society, special arrangements were made on a case by case basis with the hospital. It is now the site of the Countess of Chester hospital in Bache and serves as the main hospital for the area with 625 beds.

Despite the reputations of some institutions, most asylums in Victorian society actually marked a turning point in how we treated the mentally ill. In some asylums, it was believed that mental health issues were caused by malnutrition and dreary city life. As a result, treatment was carried out in asylums found in the countryside where people could be taken away from city life and fed well. There were doctors who did abuse their patients in asylums of course, but there seems to be little record of Cheshire County Lunatic Asylum being one of them.

In 1837 around 50,000 workers in Manchester were unemployed or were on short time due to a collapse in trade in the cotton industry. This led to widespread unrest. Falling wages and Irish immigration did not help the mood of the city. Irish immigrants accepted lower standards of living and lower wages because they were better than those on offer in Ireland. This led to the rise of Manchester Chartism and the city being known as the home of economic radicalism. In 1821 the Manchester Guardian campaigned for economic reforms that David Ricardo had put forward and the Anti-Corn Law League was found in the city. This was the home of the Manchester School of free traders.

Doctor John Snow was a pioneer of anaesthesia. He was a Victorian physician and was the doctor who provided Queen Victoria with chloroform to help her give birth to Princess Louise in 1848, Prince Leopold in 1853 and Beatrice in 1857. His first paper on the vapour of ether was published in 1847, only 3 years after he had obtained his medical degree. It is from him and his work that I have taken the method that Doctor Jones uses to pacify Sarah during their first meeting. Doctor Jones uses chloroform rather than ether to render Sarah unconscious and harmless.

Come at once if convenient. If inconvenient, come all the same is a quote from Sherlock Holmes: Adventure of the Creeping Man by Sir Arthur Conan Doyle was one of 12 short stories that were published in Strand Magazine between October 1921 and April 1927.

The Dall Estate is an estate found on Loch Rannoch and is a clan seat estate that dates back to 1347.

Book cyphers were used during the American Revolution as

well as during the Napoleonic Wars and are still used today. They feature heavily in fiction and rely on the same book and edition of that book being owned by those that are sending coded messages to each other. The bible is a common book cypher as it is widely available. Other books and texts that have been used in real-world cyphers include *the Declaration of Independence* and *Commentaries on the Laws of England*.

In 1826 improvements were made to the markets of Chester. Buildings for the markets were constructed that were ornamental as well as suitable for hosting markets inside. The fish and vegetable market were located to the south of the city, the butter market was found in the east, and the meat and poultry market was to the north. Prior to this, all the market stalls were found outside the Exchange in a rather higgledy-piggledy fashion which led to complaints. These complaints led to the creation of the new markets. For the sake of the story the market still has a feeling of a mixed chaos that includes some exotic stalls, though these are very unlikely to have ever been seen in Chester during the Victorian Era.

~*~*~

A spate of seemingly petty thefts sees the circus is taking the blame, but Lady Sarah thinks there is more to it than meets the eye. Can she prove the circus people innocent and find the culprit on her own or will the real criminal escape justice? **The Day the Circus came to Stickleback Hollow**, Book 4 in the Mysteries of Stickleback Hollow is waiting for you now.

~*~*~

Thank you for reading **Mr Daniel Cooper of Stickleback Hollow**. I hope you enjoyed it! Want to read more about the adventures of Lady Sarah? An exclusive story about them is available for free for all my newsletter subscribers. Visit **https://mailchi.mp/cea2332e3102/cs-woolley-newsletter** to

sign up and get access to it, and a whole heap of other exclusive content, offers and contests.

~*~*~

Love the Mysteries of Stickleback Hollow? Then dive into Rising Empire: Part 1, Book 1 in the Chronicles of Celadmore. *Trapped in a political marriage, a queen must fight to save her children, protect both of her kingdoms, and the man she loves, from the forces of darkness.*

~*~*~

Want to help a reader out? Reviews are crucial when it comes to helping readers choose their next book and you can help them by leaving just a few sentences about this book as a review. It doesn't have to be anything fancy, just what you liked about the book and who you think might like to read it.

Use the QR below to leave a review.

If you don't have time to leave a review or don't feel confident writing one, recommending a book to your family, friends and co-workers can help them choose their next book, so feel free to spread the word.

About the Series

Mysteries abound

When her parents die from fever, Lady Sarah Montgomery Baird Watson-Wentworth has to leave India, a land she was born and raised in, and travel to England for the first time. Finding it almost impossible to adjust to London society, Sarah flees to the county of Cheshire and the country estate of Grangeback that borders the village of Stickleback Hollow.

A place filled with oddballs, eccentrics and more suspicious characters than you can shake a stick at, Sarah feels more at home in the sleepy little village than she ever did in the big city, however, even sleepy little villages have mysteries that must be solved.

Set in Victorian England, the Mysteries of Stickleback Hollow follows the crime-solving efforts of Constable Arwyn Evans, Mr Alexander Hunter and Lady Sarah Montgomery Baird Watson-Wentworth.

From theft to murder, supernatural occurrences and missing people, Stickleback Hollow is a magical place filled with oddballs, outcasts, rogues, eccentrics and ragamuffins.

Preview from the next book
The Day the Circus Came to Stickleback Hollow

The blizzard lasted throughout the night, but by the morning, the world around Grangeback was still and quiet.

The pristine snow glistened under the rays of the rising sun and made for almost perfect riding conditions as far as Sarah was concerned.

The visit to Stickleback Hollow the previous day had left Grace in a rather desperate state, and no amount of arguing could prevent Mrs Bosworth from locking Grace in her room.

Sarah dressed and made her way down to the stables without Grace in tow. She had promised that she would go and speak to Alex about Paul Curran, but she needed to go and visit the circus first.

Black Guy was anxious to be let out of his stable after several days of being cooped up in it. The pair set off through the freshly fallen snow and across the land of Grangeback to the circus camp on the lands of Duffleton.

As Sarah approached the camp, only one of the women left to fetch the men in the tent. Rather than coming out to meet Sarah, as they had for Arwyn and Alex, they waited for her at the edge of the camp.

"Good morning, milady. What brings you out to our camp in such weather?" Bairstow asked as Sarah brought Black Guy to a halt by the three men.

"I came to talk to the ringmaster; I assume that is you," Sarah said as she looked down at the three men.

"I am. The name is Bairstow. Who are you?" the ringmaster said as Sarah dismounted.

"I am Lady Montgomery Baird Watson-Wentworth from the Grangeback estate," Sarah introduced herself as her feet touched the ground.

"A pleasure, milady. May I introduce Mr Dominic Smith and Mr Peter Libby," Bairstow pointed to the giant man first and then to the smaller one.

"Gentleman, can one of you take care of my horse whilst I talk with Mr Bairstow?" Sarah asked with a smile.

"It would be an honour," Peter bowed slightly and took Black Guy's reins from Sarah.

Bairstow led the lady into the tent that the three men

had emerged from, and Dominic remained outside to make sure that nobody went in uninvited.

"So what business is it that you wish to talk about? Missing property or Mr Paul Curran," Bairstow asked as the pair sat down.

The tent was filled with a range of costumes and boxes. A table had been made out of two barrels and a plank of wood. Sarah sat on a chest on one side of the table whilst Bairstow sat on the other.

"I have no need to ask about Mr Curran. I know where he is, and he is safe for the moment," Sarah replied. A look of panic briefly flickered over the ringmaster's face, "I came to talk to you about the missing property. All the items are small and mostly worth very little. This suggests that the thief isn't someone that is trying to profit from the theft."

"What are you saying?" Bairstow frowned.

"I think you know who the thief is and you are trying to protect them as best you can. Constable Evans doesn't believe that anything has been stolen, that the property has simply been lost. There will be no trouble from the police if the items are simply returned," Sarah replied.

"Dominic, go fetch Emily," Bairstow shouted.

"She really doesn't mean anything about it. She can't help herself. We try to make sure that she is never on her own, but she was so excited about seeing her sister that she has been running off in search of her since we arrived. When we heard people talking about things going missing, we made sure that she didn't leave the camp, but the damage had already been done," Bairstow sighed.

"Her sister?" Sarah asked.

"Yes, Grace Read," Bairstow replied, and Sarah laughed.

"I'm sorry, Grace is my maid. She has been helping me talk to the people that Emily stole from. She would be with me now; only she has been forced to stay in bed with a terrible cold," Sarah explained. The flap of the tent was pushed aside a petit blonde girl scurried in.

"Emily, this is the lady that your sister works for. She has come to take back all the things that you have stolen," Bairstow told the girl in a matter-of-fact tone.

"Am I in trouble?" Emily asked. She was a few years younger than Grace, but she was the spitting image of her sister.

"No, if you give me back everything that was taken,

then I will make sure that it is returned and that will be the end of it," Sarah assured her.

"I'll go and fetch the things," Emily said. She disappeared out of the tent.

"Can I ask, where is Paul?" Bairstow enquired nervously.

"I believe he is at the lodge on the Grangeback estate. The cook found him in the hen house, and the gamekeeper took him to the lodge and kept him from the constable." Sarah said. Relief flooded over the face of the ringmaster.

"We were hoping to hide him until we moved on; he isn't the kind of man to cause trouble or to get involved with fights," Bairstow said earnestly.

"If Mr Hunter is protecting him, then he has a good reason to," Sarah soothed.

Emily returned to the tent carrying an armful of assorted items and handed them over to Sarah.

Sarah didn't spend long in the circus camp; it wasn't even lunchtime when she arrived at the lodge and knocked on the front door.

"I'm still not letting you in, Arwyn," Alex shouted from somewhere inside the house.

"It's not Arwyn," Sarah replied. The bolt on the door was pulled back, and Mr Hunter opened the door.

"Arwyn told me what happened yesterday," Sarah said.

"Are you here to tell me to hand Paul over to the police?" Alex asked.

"I'm here to listen to why," Sarah replied.

"Then you better come in," Alex sighed.

Get your copy now!

About the Author

I was born in Macclesfield, Cheshire, UK, and raised in the nearby town of Wilmslow. From an early age I discovered I had a flair and passion for writing.

I began writing at the age of 7 and was first published in 2010. I currently live with my partner, Matt, and our two cats in Christchurch, New Zealand.

As an avid horsewoman and gamer, I also have a passion for singing, dancing, the theatre, and my garden.

Facebook: https://www.facebook.com/AuthorC.S.Woolley

Instagram: https://www.instagram.com/thecswoolley

Website: http://.mightierthantheswords worduk.com

For access to exclusive content, contests and freebies, sign up for my newsletter here https://mailchi.mp/cea2332e3102/cs-woolley-newsletter.

Also by the Same Author

The Mysteries of Stickleback Hollow

A Thief in Stickleback Hollow
All Hallows' Eve in Stickleback Hollow
Mr Daniel Cooper of Stickleback Hollow
The Day the Circus came to Stickleback Hollow
A Bonfire Surprise in Stickleback Hollow
Tinker, Tailor, Soldier, Die
What Became of Henry Cartwright
The March of the Berry Pickers
The Advent of Stickleback Hollow
Christmas in Stickleback Hollow
Spring in Stickleback Hollow
Lady de Mandeville in Stickleback Hollow
A Day Trip to Brighton
12 Days of Christmas in Stickleback Hollow
Easter in Stickleback Hollow

Chronicles of Celadmore

Rising Empire: Part 1
Rising Empire: Part 2
Rising Empire: Part 3
Rising Empire Trilogy
Shroud of Darkness
Lady of Fire
End of Days
Shroud of Darkness Trilogy

The Children of Snotingas

WYRD
HILD

The Children of Ribe

FATE
WAR
WIFRITH
DOUBT
SKÅNE
SHIPWRECKED
FEAR
HOME
The Arm Rings of Yngvar Collection
TREASON
MURDER
SEDITION
STRIFE
SUSPICION
ALLEGIANCE
DECEIT
REGICIDE
The Bergkonge Collection
BETRAYAL
JOTUNHEIMR
ALFHEIMR
NILFHEIMR
SVARTALFHEIMR
MUSPELLHEIMR
VALHALLA
RAGNAROK
The Rise of the Völvur

Further information on these titles can be found at
mightierthanthesworduk.com

Books Adapted by C.S. Woolley For Foxton Books

Level 1 400 Headwords
The Wizard of Oz by L. Frank Baum
The Adventures of Huckleberry Finn by
Mark Twain
The Adventure of the Speckled Band by
Arthur Conan Doyle
Anne of Green Gables by L. Maud
Montgomery
Dracula by Bram Stoker
The Prisoner of Zenda by Anthony
Hope
The Lost World by Arthur Conan Doyle
The Little Prince by Antonie de Saint-
Exupéry
A Little Princess by Frances Hodges
Burnett
The Secret Garden by Frances Hodges
Burnett

Level 2 600 Headwords
Moby Dick by Herman Melville
Gulliver's Travels by Jonathan Swift
Alice in Wonderland by Lewis Carroll
Sleepy Hollow by Washington Irving
Treasure Island by Robert Louis
Stevenson

Around the World in Eighty Days by
Jules Verne
Robinson Crusoe by Daniel Defoe
Beauty and the Beast by Gabrielle-
Suzanne Barbot de Villeneuve
Heidi by Johanna Spyri
The Jungle Book by Rudyard Kipling

Level 3 900 Headwords
The Three Musketeers by Alexandre
Dumas
Pocahontas by Charles Dudley Warner
Oliver Twist by Charles Dickens
Frankenstein by Mary Shelly
Journey to the Centre of the Earth by
Jules Verne
Call of the Wild by Jack London

Level 4 1300 Headwords
The Count of Monte Cristo by
Alexandre Dumas
The Merchant of Venice by William
Shakespeare
The Railway Children by Edith Nesbit
Jane Eyre by Charlotte Bronte

Level 5 1700 Headwords

The Thirty-Nine Steps by John Buchan

David Copperfield by Charles Dickens

Great Expectations by Charles Dickens

Twenty Thousand Leagues Under the

Sea by Jules Verne

Level 6 2300 Headwords

Kidnapped by Robert Louis Stevenson

The Mysterious Island by Jules Verne

Other

11 Plus Flash Cards

Acknowledgments

Writing can be an extremely lonely profession at times, but thankfully I never have to go through any of the pressures alone. My wonderful Matthew has been a source of constant support to me during all of my writing endeavours since we first met. I couldn't ask for a more fitting partner to share my life or love with.

Writing is not something I stumbled into either, my mother, Helen, took me, and my sisters, to the library every weekend when we were young to get different books, and I always maxed out the number of books I could get. Not only did she encourage me to read, but to write as well. To say I have been writing stories and poetry since I was 7 is not an exaggeration and the development of my writing career is due in no small part to her.

My mother-in-law, Lesley, has also been a source of unflinching and unwavering support, something I could not do without.

To Laura and Sam, who have read and offered opinions, death threats and encouragement on my early drafts, you are true treasures. Amy, you too are worth your weight and more in gold for all your love and support.

It may seem that writers only function alone, but I am blessed to be part of an amazing community of authors whom I know that I have helped push me to even greater heights and success. So to Quinn Ward, Donna Higton, Charlene Perry, Scarlett Braden Moss, Bryan Cohen, Chez Churton, Eliza Green, John Beresford, Rich Cook, Robert Scanlon, Jen Lassalle, Cathy MacRae, Ariella Zoella, and Helen Blenkinsop, my dear friends, thank you.

And finally, to you, dear reader, without you there would be no books, no series, no career. I want to thank you for all the time that you spend reading my work, reviewing it, sharing it with your friends and family. Without you there would be nothing. Thank you from the bottom of my heart. If you haven't already signed up for my newsletter, please do. Newsletter subscribers get access to an exclusive section of my website that is filled with additional content, free stories and contests that are not available anywhere else. To sign up, just visit https://mailchi.mp/cea2332e3102/cs-woolley-newsletter.

Until we meet again in my next book, thank you and adieu.

Made in United States
North Haven, CT
19 April 2022

18395559R00104